PRAISE FOR THE GRIMWOOD

'This book made my face hurt! Relentlessly funny.'
Rob Biddulph, author of *Peanut Jones*

'Ted and Nancy are my favourite funny foxes EVER.'
Liz Pichon, author of *Tom Gates*

'You're in for a treat!'
Selom Sunu, illustrator of *Look Both Ways*

'PURE GENIUS!'
Louie Stowell, author of *Loki: A Bad God's Guide to Being Good*

'Made us laugh out loud.'
Jim Smith, author of *Barry Loser*

'Fizzes with mad energy.'
Phil Earle, author of *When the Sky Falls*

'I CACKLED ALOUD on practically every page. Comic gold, tinged with such tenderness.'
Kiran Millwood Hargrave, author of *The Girl of Ink and Stars*

'BRILLIANTLY BONKERS, A TOTAL HOOT!'
SOPHY HENN, AUTHOR OF *PIZAZZ*

'FANTASTIC!'
LAUREN LAVERNE

'FUNNY, ANARCHIC AND GLORIOUSLY SILLY.'
RICHARD OSMAN

'Like *Watership Down*, but funny. You'll laugh hysterically on every page.' Caitlin Moran

'Nadia Shireen has done it again! *Grimwood: Let the Fur Fly!* is brilliant and super funny!'
Maisie Chan

First published in Great Britain in 2022
by Simon & Schuster UK Ltd

This paperback edition first published in 2023

1 3 5 7 9 10 8 6 4 2

Simon & Schuster UK Ltd
1st Floor, 222 Gray's Inn Road, London
WC1X 8HB

www.simonandschuster.co.uk
www.simonandschuster.com.au
www.simonandschuster.co.in

Simon & Schuster Australia, Sydney
Simon & Schuster India, New Delhi

A CIP catalogue record for this book is available from the British Library.

PB ISBN 978-1-4711-9934-9
eBook ISBN 978-1-4711-9935-6
eAudio ISBN 978-1-3985-1735-6

Printed and Bound in the UK using 100% Renewable Electricity
at CPI Group (UK) Ltd

NO REAL ANIMALS WERE HARMED
IN THE MAKING OF THIS BOOK

GRIMWOOD

LET THE FUR FLY!

NADIA SHIREEN

Simon & Schuster

A cute little fox from the Big City who thinks everything in Grimwood is amazing. He likes theatre, smelling flowers and everything being great.

Ted's older sister, a streetwise fox who thinks Grimwood is utterly bananas. She likes coffee, growling and looking after Ted.

Bouncy and ferocious, Willow the rabbit has a big heart and endless energy, but she will thwack you in the face if you call her cute, OK?

The mayor of Grimwood. Titus is a kind old stag who is good at baking and cries at soppy films about dolphins. Wants everyone to be lovely to each other.

An extremely glamorous duck who used to be in the movies. Owns a global chain of luxury hotels but currently lives on a pile of old shopping trolleys.

A grumpy owl with massive eyebrows who secretly likes everyone. He spends his evenings reading difficult novels and listening to jazz.

I'm **ERIC DYNAMITE**, and though I may look like a humble woodlouse, I am also your loyal friend and guide! How are you? Have you done something new with your hair? Now hold the end of my tiny little woodlousey hand (gently, please, I don't want it to fall off) as we embark upon A GRIMWOOD ADVENTURE. Hooray!

Oh, and if you haven't been to Grimwood before, then WORRY NOT! Because I have brought along this extremely useful map:

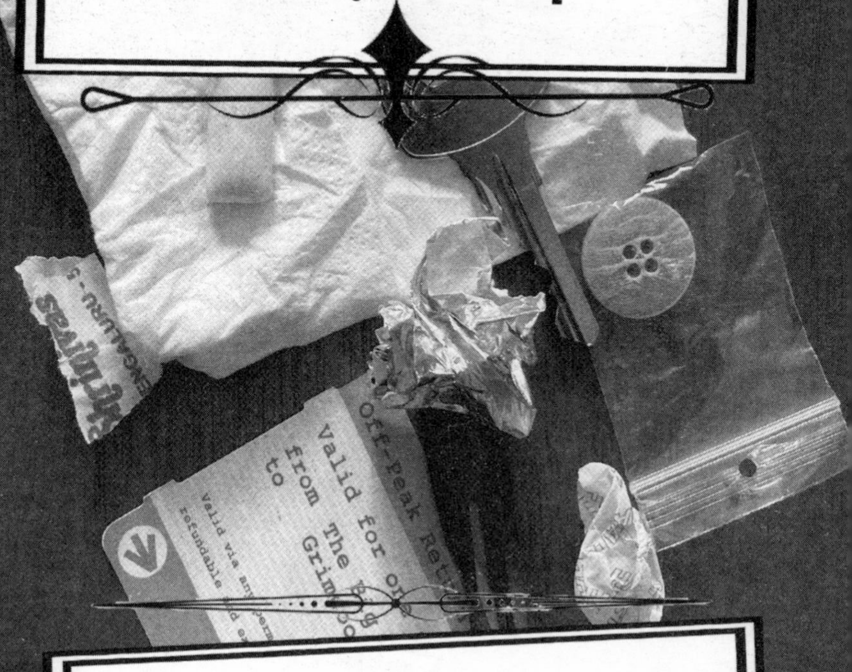

OH, no, no, no! I'm so sorry. That's actually the inside of my handbag. Um . . . can somebody sort this out, please? We were after a MAP? That's 'MAP', do you understand? A MAP.

Grimwood
Warning: Map completely useless
THE BIG CITY
BUNNYVILLE
TITUS'S CARAVAN

THAT'S more like it. Right! On with the story! Let our minds be blown, let our hearts be warmed, let our armpits be tickled. **HONK HONK!**

The Oldest Butterfly in the World
(made of crisps)

CHAPTER ONE

Ginger Fiasco takes a trip

It was a peaceful afternoon in Grimwood. The sun was shining, birds were tweeting, ants were anting and a squirrel was flying through the air at a dangerously high speed.

'Treeeebooooonk!' it screamed, before splatting into a tree trunk and slumping to the ground.

A whistle blew.

'OK, let's have a break, everyone!' hooted an owl. His name was Frank, and he was the coach of the Grimwood treebonk team. He had very large eyebrows because some owls just do.

Willow, an outrageously cute little bunny rabbit, was holding a tray of juicy orange slices for the players.

'COME ON, TEAM!' she bellowed. 'Suck on these wedges of fruity goodness! Feel the vitamins pump through your veins! I wanna see you thwacking those tree trunks MUCH harder, *capeesh*?'

The gaggle of dizzy squirrels staggered towards her. One of them was MASSIVE and had an extremely bushy tail. That was Nancy, and

she wasn't a squirrel at all. She was, in fact, a fox.

'Cheers, Willow,' she grunted, grabbing a fistful of orange.

Nancy was the only fox on Grimwood's treebonk team, but she didn't care. She wasn't *quite* as fast as the squirrels, but she was strong and her tail was powerful. It helped catapult her from tree to tree, and she was quickly becoming Grimwood's star player. Not bad for a scruffy fox from the Big City.

'Yay, go Nancy!' shouted Ted, her little brother. He waved at her from the sidelines. Treebonk really wasn't Ted's thing – he was more into acting and singing and writing poems about clouds – but he enjoyed watching his big sis practise. *Especially* if he could eat cakes at the same time.

ERIC DYNAMITE'S

Emergency Fact File:

I'm sensing you may have questions. Fear not! Your friend Eric D is here to help.

What the jiggins is Grimwood?

Grimwood is a forest far, far, faaaaar away. It is full of trees and sky and mud and stones. It smells weird and there's loads of litter and old shopping trolleys. There's a broken electricity pylon in the middle of it that buzzes strangely. But it's also FUN and GREAT and it's where this story is set so you'd better get used to it.

What the Jiminy is treebonk?

Treebonk is a woodland sport mainly played by squirrels. They jump off really tall trees and shout 'TREEEEEBONK!'. Then they boing off other trees and try not to touch the ground. They must boing for as long as possible. This goes on for absolutely ages until one team is entirely on the ground or all the players start crying.

What in the name of Jehoshaphat is an owl?

Now this is a complicated one. An OWL is a large bird with a BEAK and two massive flappy WINGS. It goes 'hoot-hoot-hoot' and can spin its head around really far, which looks cool and weird. For centuries, owls have been manufactured in a little family-run factory in Portugal.

'Gosh, just *watching* treebonk is exhausting, isn't it?' sighed Titus the stag, shovelling a jam doughnut into his snout. 'Where on earth do they find the energy?'

'No idea,' said Wiggy, whose large badgery paws were holding a jug of pink lemonade. 'Another glass of fizz, old pal?'

Titus was the mayor of Grimwood. He had big, kind eyes, knobbly antlers and a heart of love and goodness. He was also keen on baking and watching romantic comedies. Wiggy the badger often drove around Grimwood in a rusty old Jeep, but today he was relaxing next to Titus and Ted on a tatty picnic blanket.

'Did you see me give out the oranges?' panted Willow, hopping back to the picnic blanket.

'I sure did!' said Ted, and he gave her a high-five.

'Frank says if I keep doing a good job he'll give me an even bigger badge,' said Willow. 'He says I'm the best assistant coach he's ever had.'

Willow pointed to a badge she had attached to her fur. It said 'ASISTUNT COWCH'.

'You're doing a marvellous job, young Willow,' said Titus kindly. 'BAAARP! Oh, I'm so sorry. This pink fizz gives me terrible wind. BAAAARP! There I go again.'

Titus's sudden burping attack gave Ted and Willow the giggles.

Frank puffed up his chest and shouted, 'Treebonkers assemble!'

The team lined themselves up.

'We're *really* going to go for it this time,' said Frank. 'Ready? One . . . two . . . three . . .

TTRREEEEEBOOOOOOOONK!'

The sky grew dark as squirrels flew through the air, boinging and bouncing their way around the treebonk pitch – a clearing surrounded by a circle of tall pine trees.

THUNK! Two squirrels collided in mid-air. One managed to boing against a branch, but the other plummeted to the ground.

BA-ZOINGGGGG! Nancy used her powerful tail to ricochet through some gnarly branches, her paws never once touching the ground. She laughed as she went. It reminded her of being on the run with her foxy pals back in the Big City, hopping over bus stops and rooftops with a bag of chips in her mouth.

POINGGG! An overexcited squirrel called Ginger Fiasco lost control of her steering and treebonked herself right out of the pitch.

'Uh-oh,' said Wiggy. Everyone looked up and watched Ginger fly high across the sky like a furry rocket.

'Where will she land?' wondered Titus.

Everything went quiet.

And then faintly . . . very faintly . . . they heard an angry quack.

'Oh, phew,' said Willow. 'She's just landed in the Small Pond.'

The Small Pond was home to many creatures, but mainly Ingrid – a very important and powerful duck.

Frank spun his head around to face the picnickers. 'Don't suppose one of you lot fancies getting off your bottom and bringing back Ginger?' he asked. 'She's always knocked out cold when this happens.'

'I'll go!' said Ted, slinging his rucksack over his shoulder.

'Good laddie,' said Frank. He turned to Titus and Wiggy to tell them off for being lazy, but they had both nodded off in their deckchairs.

Nancy noticed Ted walking towards the Small Pond. When they had first arrived in

Grimwood she would never have let him go off on his own. But Grimwood was their home now, and Nancy knew her little brother would come to no harm in these deep, dark woods.

Apparently if you turn the page
the story just . . . carries on!
Marvellous inventions, these
'books', don't you think?

CHAPTER TWO
Ted goes a-windering and a-wandering

Ted chuckled to himself as he pranced through the woods. There hadn't been a dull moment since he and Nancy had moved to Grimwood. If he wasn't saving injured squirrels, he was helping Titus make Crazyhorns Power Juice, going for bumpy car rides with Wiggy or starring in shows with Ingrid's theatre group, the Grimwood Players.

He was a very happy little fox, but (and be warned, because this is quite a big BUT) he wished he knew where his mum and dad were.

They had left Ted and Nancy all alone as little cubs, in a park in the Big City. Ted didn't know why. Nancy had looked after him ever since. And even though the cubs had settled in Grimwood, Ted still wrote letters to their parents and posted them back to their old den in the Big City. Just in case.

Dear Mum and Dad

Nancy is getting SO GOOD at treebonk! Frank reckons she is 'a natural'. Oh, and do you remember the mayor, Titus? Well, I've been helping him with his new recipe for Crazyhorns Power Juice. It's got nettles in, and it tastes disgusting, so I might chuck in some lemonade when he's not looking.

Willow is still my very best friend. These are our latest hobbies:

1. Doing dance routines
2. Making daisy chains
3. Running around laughing

Ingrid the duck is really grumpy at the moment because Pamela accidentally blew up her stage. Remember Pamela? The weird eagle who's always blowing stuff up? Anyway, it means no more rehearsals for our theatre group, the Grimwood Players. BOO!

I miss you both loads. Nancy doesn't say it much, but I know she misses you too. I am so tall now that I reach her armpit. I wish you could see. It would be nice to know what you look like, too. And maybe have some cuddles! (When nobody is looking Nancy lets me cuddle her, which is nice.) Anyway, I have to go because Willow wants us to look for pebbles that look like faces. I have drawn another map in case you want to find us.

I love you
Ted xx

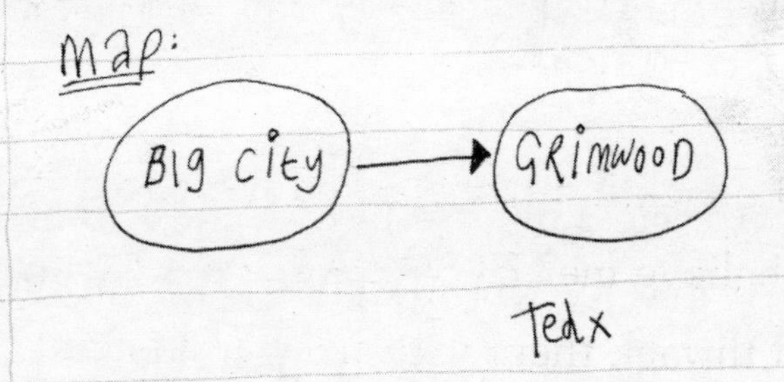

When Ted arrived at the Small Pond, Ingrid was sitting on top of a very dizzy squirrel on an island in the middle of the murky water. The rumour was that in the olden days, when Ingrid was a mere child of a duck,* she had been a glamorous movie star. 'It is entirely true!' she

would quack if anyone asked her about it. 'You don't believe me? HOW DARE YOU!' Then she would thwack them with her handbag, to show how annoyed she was.

*Pretty sure we call those 'ducklings'.

'Tell the owl to keep his ridiculous tree-bonkers under control!' shrieked Ingrid, flapping her wings in annoyance. 'This squirrel landed on my nest while I was putting on my eye make-up and NOW LOOK AT ME.'

'Sorry, Ingrid,' said Ted, expertly hopping from one shopping trolley to another until he reached them. He lifted Ginger by the tail, shoved an orange slice in her mouth and plopped her into his rucksack. 'I can't wait for the Grimwood Players to start meeting again! When do rehearsals begin?'

Ingrid sighed dramatically and brought an elegant wing to her brow. 'Darlink, I just cannot find the va-va-voom to carry on. Not since the destruction of our beautiful theatre. SOB!'

'I'm sure we can build a new theatre, Ingrid,' said Ted brightly.

But Ingrid just sighed.

'I've lost my inspiration,' she said. 'And what good is an actor without inspiration? What is a duck without her quack? Oh! I despair, how I despaaaaaaaair.'

And she snapped on a silk eye mask and waddled back to her boudoir.

'Bye then!' said Ted. He bounded through

the forest with Ginger safely tucked inside his rucksack, sniffing the slightly eggy smell that sometimes wafted through the air and hopping over some discarded tyres. Soon, he found himself in Bunnyville, which was a village full of cows. Not really, it was full of bunnies, don't be silly. There were hundreds of them boinging about all over the place.

'Hi, Ted!' said about fifty of them at the same time.

'Hiya!' said Ted. He noticed a big pile of grey squishy mattresses. The bunnies were climbing high up into the branches of an extremely tall pine tree and leaping off like it was a massive diving board . . . before BOINGING onto the mattresses. It looked like great fun.

'A hoomin must have just dumped them here,' squeaked Tyler, who Ted recognized as one of Willow's 147 brothers. 'It's brilliant!'

Tyler hitched up his shorts, wiped his nose on his paw and scampered back up the tree.

Ted chuckled to himself and carried on through Grimwood. But as the trees crowded around him, he started to feel just a tiny bit . . . well, not scared, exactly. Things just looked darker all of a sudden. And, apart from the dozy squirrel in his rucksack, Ted suddenly felt a little bit *too* alone.

So, he started to sing a song to himself, which was a very Ted thing to do.

Just hoppin' through the forest
It's a nice and friendly place
Nuthin's gonna get me
Or try and bite my face

The trees are nice and branchy
And just because it's dark
Nuthin's gonna get me
Else I'll do a great big bark . . .

'What a *marvellous* tune,' said a voice in the darkness.

'ARGH!' screamed Ted, and he turned to run but crashed straight into a tree trunk. He sat up and rubbed his nose.

'Wh . . . who's there?' he whimpered. 'Frank? Is that you? Nance? Nance!'

He heard some leaves crunching nearby.

'Don't be alarmed, little one,' said the voice. 'I'm not going to hurt you.'

And then Ted saw something move. A tall shadow; two large, pointy ears. And, just for a moment, a glint of silver.

'Wh . . . who are you?' Ted whispered into the darkness.

And then something grabbed his tail.

CHAPTER THREE
The shadow

Ted yelped as he was hoisted up by his tail. 'Put me down, put me DOWN!' he squealed.

Whoever had grabbed Ted let go of him. He landed on the ground with a great big BONK, which made him go dizzy.

He stood up cautiously while staring at the tall stranger. He could just about make out two very pointy ears, a snout and a big, bushy tail . . .

'You're a fox!' he gasped.

The mysterious figure quickly stepped back further into the shadows.

'Tell me, lad,' said the voice, which was deep and smooth. 'Where are we?'

Ted looked confused.

'Erm . . . Grimwood,' he said.

'Ah, yes, Grimwood! Just as I thought,' said the voice.

'Who *are* you?' asked Ted, feeling braver now that he hadn't been eaten.

'Who, me? Oh, nobody,' chuckled the voice. 'Now tell me. That large metal tower you have in . . . *Grimwood*. What is it, exactly?'

'Oh, well, *that* is the Magic Tower,' said Ted. 'In the Big City we would have just called it an electricity pylon. But the Magic Tower is kind of different. It's a bit broken, cos it's got loose cables hanging off it and it's always making a buzzing noise. And you *definitely* shouldn't chew on the electricity cables cos it's dangerous and you would *totally* die. Even though Pamela does. But then Pamela is also dangerous.'

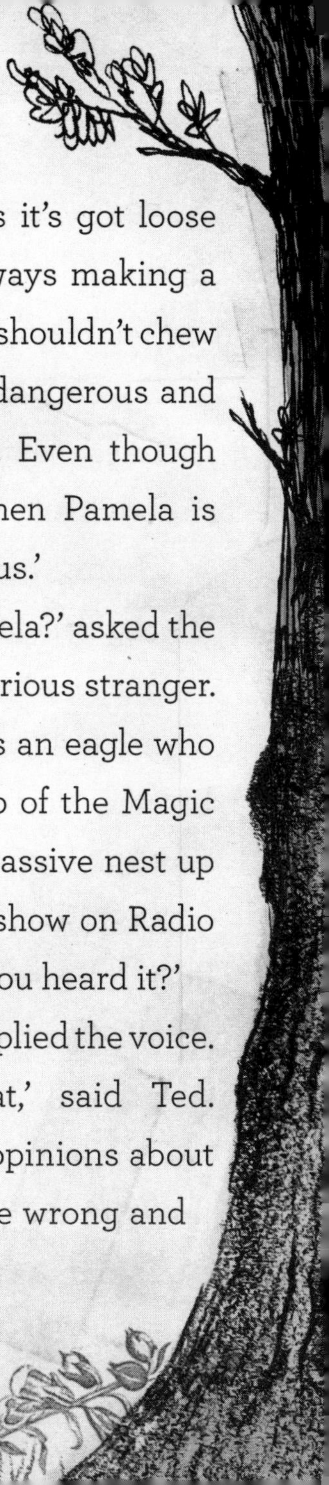

'Pamela?' asked the mysterious stranger.

'Yeah, she's an eagle who lives at the top of the Magic Tower. Got a massive nest up there. She does a show on Radio Grimwood. Have you heard it?'

'I have not,' replied the voice.

'Oh, it's great,' said Ted. 'People call in and tell her their opinions about things, she tells them that they're wrong and then she plays a song. It's fun!'

'I'll tune in,' said the voice. 'So . . . this "Magic Tower". Gives off electricity, does it?'

Ted scratched at his snout. 'I suppose so, yeah . . . It gives *something* off, all right. I think it makes the bunnies bouncier, and the squirrels treebonkier, and Grimwood smellier . . .'

'Hmm,' pondered the mysterious stranger. 'So, it gives off *lots* of electricity?'

Ted nodded. 'Oh yes, I'd say so,' he replied. 'It's MEGA SUPER powerful.'

'How fascinating,' said the voice. 'I must take a look at it.'

'Oh, that'll be dead tricky!' said Ted. 'Pamela doesn't let *any* strangers near the Magic Tower.'

'Or what?' asked the voice.

'Er, well,' said Ted. 'Or she might bite your head off. She's done it a few times now. It's pretty brutal!'

'Goodness me.'

'Yeah! She's pretty scary if you don't know her,' said Ted. 'Actually, she's pretty scary even if you *do* know her.'

'I see.'

Ted suddenly felt a bit nervous. Something about all this seemed a bit . . . odd.

'I suppose I'd better be going,' he mumbled. 'I'm not really allowed to talk to strangers. And my big sis will be wondering where I am.'

'Yes, of course. Quite right,' said the voice. 'Goodbye then, little fox.'

'Oh, but ARE you a big fox, then? Just quickly tell me, tell me, pleeeeease!' begged Ted. And he suddenly so *desperately* wanted to see the stranger that he scrambled forwards, tripped over some tree roots and fell down again.

When he looked up, the stranger had gone.

Ted rubbed his eyes. Had he met a real-life grown-up fox? Had that really happened?

'Oh yes,' said Ginger Fiasco, the squirrel in Ted's rucksack. She had woken up and was eating a packet of Cheesy Snackos. 'That really happened, all right.'

Suddenly, the sky went dark. There was a terrifyingly loud noise, like thunder, overhead.

CHOP-CHOP-CHOP-CHOP!

Ted and Ginger Fiasco covered their ears and scrunched their eyes shut as a great gust of wind blew over them.

The trees swayed violently, and grass and leaves flattened themselves to the earth.

'What . . . is . . . going . . . on?!' yelled Ted.

CHOP-CHOP-CHOP-CHOP-chop-chop-ch . . .

After a few seconds, the noise faded, the wind died down and the forest stopped shaking. Ted dusted himself down.

'Holy banana!' he said. 'I met another fox! An actual real-life fox!'

And, with Ginger Fiasco safely nestled in his rucksack, Ted ran back to tell the others as fast as a greasy puma.

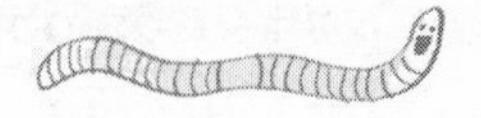

Nancy and the rest of the Treebonk team had finished their practice session by the time Ted got back. Now they were doing squirrel yoga and drinking Crazyhorns Power Juice.

'What took you so long, bro?' barked Nancy.

Ginger Fiasco crawled out of Ted's rucksack, still clutching her bag of Cheesy Snackos. 'You ain't gonna believe it,' she squeaked. And she was about to tell everyone what had happened when she fainted from eating too many Cheesy Snackos.

'I think I saw a fox!' Ted panted. 'A big one!'

Nancy looked worried and grabbed him, examining his fur and checking his ears. 'Did it hurt you?' she asked. 'Cos if anything hurts you, I'm gonna dead it right up.'

Ted shook his head. 'No, he didn't hurt me, sis. Well, he grabbed me by the tail for a bit, but it's fine.'

Willow balled her fluffy bunny paws into tiny fists.

'I'm gonna totally knock his block off an' all!' she yelled.

'PLEASE,' shouted Ted. 'I'm fine and you don't need to beat up anyone. He was this tall grown-up fox. And he smelled really nice, like old books and apple crumble.'

Nancy frowned. She looked at Titus.

'Well?' she said. 'Who is this guy? Any ideas?'

Titus shrugged. 'Honestly, my dear, I'm as baffled as you are! Biffled, buffled and indeed baffled.'

Nancy scowled.

'You told me you didn't know any other foxes,' she said.

'That's right, I don't,' replied Titus. 'But beyond Grimwood, well, who knows? I suppose it's not *impossible* that there are other foxes around.'

Ted jumped up and down impatiently.

'Where, Titus?' he asked. 'If there are other places nearby where foxes live, well then . . .'

'Well, what?' said Titus, suddenly looking quite worried.

'Maybe . . . maybe they know Mum and Dad,' said Ted quietly.

Nancy didn't say anything, and looked at her feet.

'Oh, Ted,' sighed Titus gently. 'Who knows what you *actually* saw. Looks like you've had quite the bump, there.'

Ted put a paw to his head and felt a lump just above his right eye.

'But I didn't imagine any of this, Titus,' he protested. 'Just ask Ginger Fiasco. She heard the whole thing, didn't you, Ginger?'

But Ginger was still face down in a pile of leaves, snoring extremely loudly, so she wasn't much help at all.

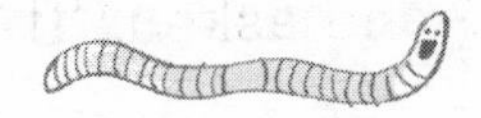

Ted and Nancy trudged back to their den. Ted was sniffling and rubbing at the bump on his head.

'Oh man, stop blubbing,' said Nancy. 'Everything's fine. You just bumped your head, innit?'

Ted kept sniffling.

Nancy sighed. She was a toughie. But she was also a good big sister. When they got inside, she tucked Ted into bed, made him a hot chocolate and handed him Slipper, which was an old slipper Ted had been cuddling since he was a tiny cub. It was one of the few things they still had from their home in the Big City.

Ted buried his face into Slipper while Nancy sat quietly beside him.

'At first I thought . . . I thought maybe it was Dad,' sniffled Ted, a little while later.

Nancy gave Ted's head a stroke.

'I've never seen a grown-up fox before,' he said.

Nancy didn't say anything for a while.

'Ted,' she said eventually. 'The thing is, I can't really remember what Mum and Dad look like. And that's really sad, but . . . I look after you all right, don't I? We don't need anyone else.'

Ted wrapped his arms around Slipper.

'Do you think they're out there somewhere?' he asked.

'I dunno,' sighed Nancy.

'Maybe they're looking for us?' he asked hopefully.

'I dunno.'

'Do you think they just . . . forgot about us?'

Nancy turned to face Ted. 'Never,' she said. 'If they can't get to us it's because . . . well, something stopped them. But they wouldn't have left us behind on purpose, Ted. I know that in my bones.'

CHEERFUL INTERLUDE
Willow, meanwhile, hopped all the way home. She did some disco dancing, ate a load of cream buns, had a bath and then went to sleep and had a dream about puffins. Woo-hoo!
CHEERFUL INTERLUDE ENDS

CHAPTER FOUR
The crow who fell to Earth

It was the middle of the night, and the sky above Grimwood was inky black, splattered with bright white stars. All was quiet.

Ted was sitting outside, snuggled under a blanket. Next to him lay his notebook, a pencil, a flask of hot tea and a load of old toilet rolls stuck together with sticky tape. He picked up the long, wobbly tube and looked up at the sky with it.

'Oi,' barked Nancy. 'What you doing with those old bog rolls?'

'It's my new telescope,' said Ted proudly. 'I'm stargazing.'

Nancy frowned up at the sky. She was still unsure about stars. In the Big City you didn't see them much, what with all the smoke and smog. She worried that they might fall down from the sky and land on her head – but she kept that to herself. Nancy liked to look hard and tough at all times, and definitely not like someone who was a bit scared of stars.

'Oooh, look!' squeaked Ted, pointing a paw at the sky. 'There's the **Big Dipper** . . . there's . . . the **chicken nugget** . . . and there's . . . the **wonky paperclip**.'

'Let me have a go on that thing then,' said Nancy, nodding at Ted's bog-roll telescope.

Ted handed it over.

As Nancy peered through it she fell silent. The stars *were* kind of beautiful, she had to admit.

'No matter who you are or where you live, we all look at the same stars,' said Ted dreamily. 'I like thinking about that.'

But Nancy didn't reply, as she was distracted by a particularly shiny star. It was so bright it seemed to be flashing. It also seemed to be moving.

'Ted,' she said. 'Look up at that one.'

Ted squinted.

'WOAH!' he cried out. 'A shooting star!'

'And it's shooting this way,' said Nancy, her fur standing on end.

The mysterious ball of light *did* seem to be whizzing closer and closer, and getting faster and faster. In fact . . . it was going to crash right into Grimwood!

'AAAARGH!' yelped Ted.

Without thinking, Nancy wrapped her tail around her little brother and bundled him to the ground.

There was an enormous **BANG**.

The sky flashed bright white for a moment, then went dark. After a few seconds of silence, Nancy leapt to her feet.

Then there was a noise. It sounded like muffled shouting.

'Over there,' she growled. 'Come on.'

She lifted Ted by the scruff of his neck and dragged him along as she ran towards the noise.

'B-b-but, Nance,' whimpered Ted, who was sliiiiiiightly less brave than his big sis. 'We don't know who that is. Or WHAT it is! What if it's something *unfriendly*?'

Nancy didn't stop to answer. They darted through the forest, leaping over the fallen trees and thickets of undergrowth.

They heard the noise again, louder this time.

'. . . **ooga!**'

'. . . **OOOOOOOGA!!!**'

The foxes peered into the near darkness.

'Hello?' shouted Nancy.

'**AWOOOOOOOOOOGAAAAAAAAAAAAAAA!**'

Ted and Nancy gasped. They would recognize that **awooga** anywhere.

'It's Sharon the Party Crow!' they chanted and, on hearing her name, Sharon managed to feebly wave a neon glowstick in the air.

The foxes knew Sharon the Party Crow from the Big City. She was a party LEGEND and could start a shindig anytime, anywhere.

Once, she'd held a rave by the Speedy Chicken bins that went on for so long a pigeon grew a beard. She could let off a dozen party poppers with her beak in one go.*

Another time she started a conga line that was so long it ended up in Antarctica. Nobody could party harder than Sharon. However, *now* she seemed to be stuck upside down in the branches of a beech tree.

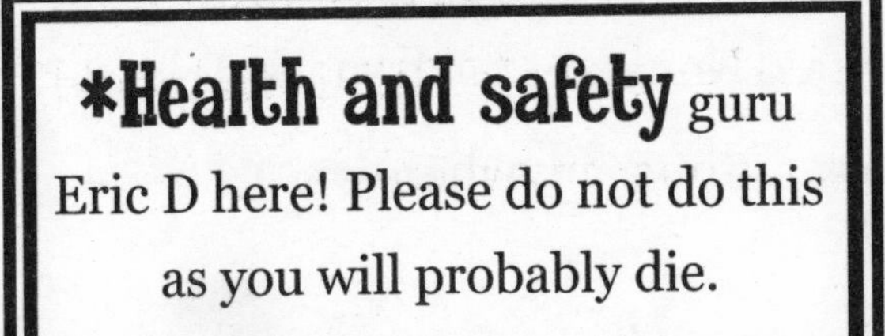

***Health and safety** guru Eric D here! Please do not do this as you will probably die.

'Party time . . . in trouble!' squawked Sharon, as Ted and Nancy hurried towards her.

Ted took off his scarf.

'Sharon!' he yelped. 'It's me, Ted! The little fox from the Big City, remember?'

Sharon nodded and gave a mournful honk on her kazoo.

'Grab hold of my scarf when I throw it, OK?' he said.

Ted twirled the scarf over his head a few times, then flung one end of it towards Sharon, who just about managed to grab it with her beak. Nancy and Ted gently pulled her out from the tangle of branches and caught her as she fell. The whole time, Sharon parped sadly on her kazoo.

'Where am I? **AWOOOOGA!**' said Sharon.

'Grimwood,' said Nancy. 'How the heck did you get here from the Big City? That's miles away.'

Sharon adjusted her glittery party hat. She also had a glittery beak, glittery feathers and glittery feet. Basically, there was a lot of glitter.

'I was at a massive party in Twinklenuts Forest! They shot me out of a glitter cannon and now I am here. I have no idea what is happening. So let's dance! **AWOOGA!**'

'What's Twinklenuts Forest?!!' asked Ted, his eyes growing big.

'You don't know Twinklenuts Forest?' said Sharon.

'NO!' shouted Ted and Nancy.

'Twinklenuts Forest! It is great! It looks like here, but much nicer. And without the smell of rotten pants. And everyone who lives there is good-looking and smells nice. **AWOOOGA!** Now dance like a robot!' And she started breakdancing.

Ted looked at Nancy with big, bright eyes.

'Nance! Did you hear that? Twinklenuts Forest! There IS somewhere else! Maybe that's where the mystery fox is from?'

Nancy felt a shiver of excitement. She had been a natural explorer back in the Big City. She'd given up roaming around when they moved to Grimwood, but now she realized she kinda missed it.

'Sharon,' said Ted. 'Where is this Twinklenuts place?'

Sharon scratched at her beak, and more glitter fell to the floor. 'Hmm, I must think. It is all so hazy . . . I remember the stretch limo . . . then a private jet. There was a handsome monkey called Diego . . . he fed me crumpets and called me beautiful. What else, what else? Oh, it is a crazy blur. At some point I think I shaved the eyebrows off a chicken called Mary. Oh, and the fairy lights! So many pretty fairy lights, la la laaaaaaa!'

'Blimey,' said Ted.

Nancy stared at Sharon for a while, who was staggering around raining glitter onto the ground.

'I think I know how we find Twinklenuts Forest,' she grinned.

CHAPTER FIVE
Swamp-hoppin'

Pamela sat in her nest at the top of the Magic Tower. She adjusted her night-vision goggles.

'Ha!' she squawked. 'Finally, I have eagle-eyed vision!'

Which was a weird thing to say, given that she was an eagle.

She fiddled about with all the junk she had collected in her nest: old wires, bits of mobile phones and radios. She found a rusty walkie-talkie and pressed the button. It screeched and buzzed to life.

'Agent Pamela reporting for duty,' she squawked. 'No alien life detected. Lasagne for dinner. Quite tasty. Over and out.'

She continued to scan the skies, hoping to see something unusual.

Then she saw the flash and glow of Sharon the Party Crow crashing into Grimwood.

'Invaders!' she cried. She adjusted her goggles and saw Ted and Nancy running over to help Sharon down from the tree.

'Hmm, the orange furries do not seem alarmed,' she said. 'Interesting.'

Then she fiddled with some complicated-looking radio equipment and put some headphones on. Thanks to a higgledy-piggledy network of microphones she had hidden all over Grimwood, she was now able to hear their conversation perfectly.

'A *party crow*? A glitter cannon?!' she gasped. 'I must meet this bird at ONCE.'

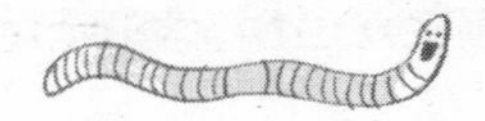

After a nap, breakfast and a bath in an empty butter dish (for Sharon, at least), Ted and Nancy set off on the hunt for Twinklenuts.

Ted ran after his big sister, trying to keep up. Sharon the Party Crow was sitting in his rucksack, honking on a kazoo every couple of seconds.

'Where are we going, Nance?' panted Ted.

Nancy pointed at the ground.

'We're following the glitter trail,' she said.

Ted looked down and saw a messy line of colourful sparkles. It was glitter that had fallen from Sharon as she had been blasted through the air.

'OI!' shouted someone from behind a large mushroom. 'Where are you lot going without me?'

It was Willow. She was knee-deep in Cosmic Knobblers, her fave forest snack (even though they made her parp uncontrollably). Ted told her everything really quickly so don't worry, we won't have to go through it all again.

The glitter led them past Bunnyville. They stopped for a bit and watched hundreds of small furry rabbits flinging themselves off the top of the very tall tree onto the pile of mattresses.

'It's the most exciting thing that's happened in ages,' said Willow. 'Well, since the waterslide we made out of dustbin lids, at least.'

'Guys, look,' said Ted, pointing at the path of glitter ahead of them.

Everyone looked up and moaned. They were heading straight for the Swamp of Despair.

The Swamp of Despair was a horrible smelly swamp on the outskirts of Grimwood. It was impossible to cross, because if you stepped on it, you'd get sucked down into gloopy, sloopy mud. Nancy had fallen into it once and had almost come to a very sticky end.

Sharon's glittery sparkles had mixed in with all the mud.

'Look, it's turned into a disco mud pit!' hooted Ted.

'Yeah, and we'd still die if we fell in,' said Nancy.

'AHA!' shouted Willow, bouncing up and down. 'I gots a plan, I gots a plan! Let's use the mattresses! We could pile them high and then do a massive BOUNCE right over this stinky old swamp.'

'Great idea!' said Ted, hopping from foot to foot.

Nancy scratched at her snout for a while.

'Your plan might not be *entirely* useless,' she said. 'We could use them like, you know, stepping stones.'

'But all those mattresses look really heavy *and* they're covered in bunnies,' said Ted.

'I know someone who can help,' said Nancy, with a grin.

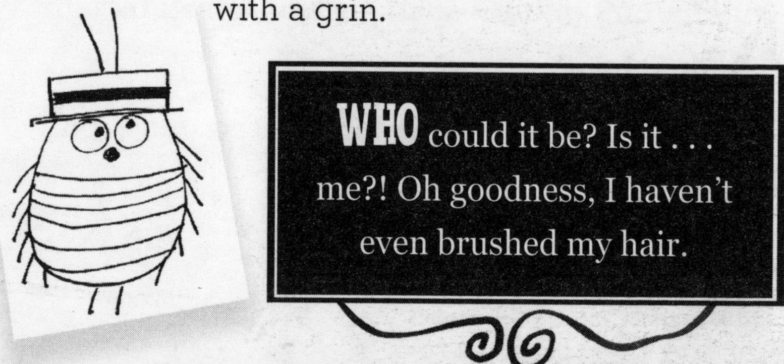

Wiggy the badger revved the engine of his Jeep. Behind him, a long, thick rope had been lashed around the tall pile of mattresses. About a squillion excited bunnies were holding the mattresses together like a tangle of furry elastic bands. It was quite a sight.

Wiggy honked his horn.

Willow stood at the very top of the pile of bunnies, holding a megaphone.

'TUCK IN YOUR EARS AND
DON'T LOOK DOWN!'
she bellowed.

She gave Wiggy the thumbs up.

The wheels of the Jeep skidded in the mud.

'HEAVE-HO!' cried Willow. 'COME ON, EVERYBODY! LET'S GET MOVING!'

A thousand tiny paws scrabbled until slowly but surely, the pile of mattresses started to move.

Ted and Nancy sat in the back of the Jeep and looked behind them. The gigantic clump of bunnies, as big as a house, was being dragged through the woods. The rabbits began to scream and hoot in excitement.

'Faster!' they yelled. 'Make it go faster!'

'I can't watch!' whimpered Ted through his paws. 'Someone's going to get hurt!'

Please can someone inform health and safety? This is ridiculous. Hang on. Am *I* health and safety? **Oh no . . .**

Soon they reached the Swamp of Despair.

The bunnies loosened the ropes and then dropped to the ground, cheering.

'That was the best fun EVER!' whooped Jacko, one of Willow's 276 siblings. 'Again, again!'

Willow stood on the bonnet of Wiggy's Jeep.

'NOW, EVERYONE, CHUCK A MATTRESS AS HARD AS YOU CAN ONTO THIS HORRIBLE SWAMP,' she shouted.

'Hooray!!!' yelled the bunnies, who were up for anything.

Soon, the mattresses were floating on the surface of the swamp like giant marshmallows in a sea of glittery hot chocolate.

Nancy jumped onto the closest mattress. It wobbled and sank a little deeper into the mud. But then it held firm. Nancy looked up and grinned.

'It's working!' she yelled to the others. 'Come on!'

But then, all chaos broke loose. There was a mighty **PCKAAAAAAAW**, and Pamela the eagle swooped down from the sky.

Willow just grinned and gave her a high-five.

''Sup, Pamela?' she asked. 'Been enjoying the radio show, dude.'

Pamela had landed on top of Wiggy's Jeep. Her head bobbed as she looked around, searching for something. Finally, she pointed a wing at Sharon the Party Crow, who was politely sitting in Ted's rucksack.

'I have come for you,' said Pamela.

'Awooga!' exclaimed Sharon excitedly.

'Sharon, meet Pamela,' said Willow. 'Pamela, meet Sharon. You're both . . . really . . . weird.'

'Do you like explosions?' asked Pamela.

'I love explosions!' hooted Sharon. 'Do you like parties?'

'I love parties!' cried Pamela.

Everyone felt a buzz of cosmic energy as the birds looked at each other.

'Join me,' said Pamela. 'We will become friends and take over the world.'

Sharon nodded and blew on her kazoo. She breakdanced over to the eagle. Then the birds shrieked and squawked and flapped their wings for a bit, before leaping into the air and flying back to the Magic Tower.

'A *very* dangerous friendship has just been formed,' sighed Willow.

'Bye then, Sharon,' said Ted, staring at the two specks in the sky.

'OI! Forget about those nutty birds. This way!' shouted Nancy, who was halfway across the swamp by now.

They all boinged from mattress to mattress like ping pong balls, trying very hard to not fall into the mud.

Willow looked up and saw that her mattress was bumping against a grassy bank. They had made it safely across the swamp. She cartwheeled onto solid ground.

'I'm a genius,' she sang, 'a total geeeenius.'

'SHHHH!' shhhh'd Nancy. 'Whoever lives

here might not be super-friendly, all right? Stay quiet.'

Everyone crouched behind some bushes.

'What now?' asked Ted.

'We listen for clues,' hissed Nancy.

They listened as hard as they could. Willow gritted her teeth and tried to make her ears go *extra* big.

Soon, they heard faint sounds: music, voices and some light, tinkling noises. And then there was a familiar smell . . .

Nancy and Ted's tails shot up at once.

There was no mistaking it.

'HOT DOGS!' they hooted, entirely forgetting the bit about being quiet.

'Er, Ted,' said Willow. 'Your eyes have gone all funny. And why are you dribbling?'

Ted grabbed Willow by the shoulders.

'HOT DOGS,' he panted. 'HOT . . . DOGS!'

'Oooookaaaaaaay,' said Willow, taking a step backwards.

'Come on,' hissed Nancy, lying on the ground. 'Stay low, everyone.' Then she started crawling along on her knees and elbows, like a soldier. Everyone copied her.

Willow giggled.

'What is it?' whispered Ted.

'I can see your bum,' said Willow.

Ted giggled too.

The gang shuffled on their bellies through the deep, dark woods. Every now and then, they spotted something unusual, like:

1. Some empty party poppers
2. A twisted-up pair of fancy-dress angel wings
3. A top hat
4. A cardboard box that said 'BERTIE WAFFLE'S BIG FALAFELS'
5. A jester hat and juggling balls

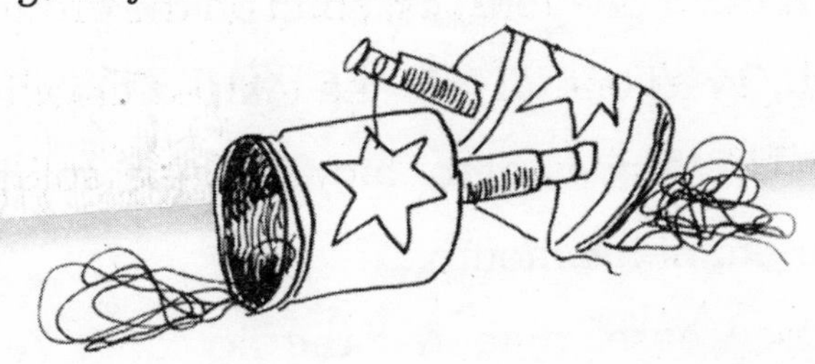

Nancy sniffed the air. The smell of sizzling onions was getting stronger. The music and talking got louder.

'Guys,' she hissed. 'Don't make a sound or any sudden moves, got it?'

'Got it,' whispered Willow.

'Got it,' whispered Wiggy.

'HOTTTTTT DOOOOOOOOOOOGS!' yelled Ted.

'Ted, no!' shouted Nancy, but it was too late. Ted was standing next to a shiny food van, panting. A confused-looking weasel in a baseball cap was staring at him from behind the counter.

'What can I get you?' asked the weasel.

'HOT DOG WITH MUSTARD, KETCHUP AND EXTRA ONIONS PLEASE!' blurted out Ted, his tongue hanging out of his mouth.

As the weasel prepared the hot dog, Ted's breathing slowed down. He gradually realized:

1. Who he was
2. Where he was
3. That Nancy had told him not to make a sound or any sudden moves

4. That he had just made lots of sounds and sudden moves
5. That Nancy was standing next to him, growling

'Oh no!' said Ted, smacking his forehead. 'I've done it again!'

'I'm sorry, Nance,' whimpered Ted. 'I couldn't help it!'

'Here you go,' said the weasel, handing over the hot dog.

'We ain't got no money,' snapped Nancy.

The weasel chuckled.

'I don't want any money, love,' she said gently. 'It's Twinklefest! Everything is free. Here, I'll make you some more.'

Ted ate the hot dog in two bites, groaning in delight.

The weasel handed over more hot dogs, and this time it was Willow, Wiggy and Nancy's turn to scoff theirs down.

'Are we in Twinklenuts?' asked Nancy.

'You sure are!' said the weasel. 'Who's for a glass of fizzy orange?'

'Gosh,' said Wiggy. 'This is absolutely *marvellous*!'

The weasel passed over four cups of fizzy orange, each with ice and a straw. The gang guzzled the drinks in one go.

'Right, burping contest,' announced Willow. 'Ready, aim, FIRE!'

'Buuuuuuuurp!'

'BAAAAAARP!'

'BeeeeoooOOOWWWWWCH!'

'BAAAUUUUUURPPPPP!'

'You lot are so childish,' said Nancy, but even she couldn't help giggling as they all rolled around on the grass, burping their heads off.

Suddenly a tall figure loomed over them, blocking out the sun.

'Well, well, well,' it said. 'What do we have here?'

Ted gasped.

Because it was a fox. A tall and handsome one, with streaks of dazzling silver running through his fur. He wore a smart tweed jacket, and his eyes were shiny and bright. His tail was luxurious and thick, not scraggly and rough like Ted and Nancy's.

'Allow me to introduce myself,' purred the fox. 'Sebastian Silver, Mayor of Twinklenuts Forest. And who on earth are you lot?'

CHAPTER SIX
Holy Twinklenuts!

Wiggy was a well-mannered badger, so he immediately stood up and dusted himself down.

'Wigthorpe Barrington Mario Sinclair, though everyone calls me Wiggy. DELIGHTED to make your acquaintance, sir!'

He took Sebastian Silver's paw in his own and pumped it up and down vigorously.

'Charmed,' said Sebastian Silver, gently pulling his arm away.

Ted's mouth hung open.

'It's you!' he said. 'You're him! I met you, like, yesterday!'

Sebastian Silver looked down at Ted, frowning. Then he quickly gave a big grin.

'Oh yes!' he said. 'So, you somehow found your way over to Twinklenuts, eh? All the way from that funny little place you live in. Well, how *wonderful* to have you here.'

Willow shoved herself in front of Sebastian and held out a stout paw.

'I'm Willow,' she said. 'I'm very cool and brilliant but don't ever call me cute, all right?'

Sebastian chuckled and gave a small bow.

'I wouldn't dream of it,' he said. 'Remind me, what's your little patch called again? Grizzletown, was it?'

'Grimwood,' said Wiggy.

'We're right next door to you!' said Willow. 'We've had the Swamp of Despair between us all this time. But thanks to my GREAT idea, we managed to bounce across it! YAY ME.' She beamed proudly.

Sebastian Silver was quiet for a moment. 'I see,' he said after a while. 'And indeed, "Yay, you", little bunny. Do you know, in all this time, I didn't know anyone actually lived *there*. Anyway! Let me show you around my humble little home.'

He led them through a cluster of trees, up a grassy bank and down a peaceful footpath. His shiny tail swished as he walked and the silver streaks in his fur flashed in the sunshine, looking very fancy.

'Welcome to Twinklenuts!' said Sebastian Silver, and he stretched out his arms.

Ted, Nancy, Willow and Wiggy stood in silence and stared. It was so pretty. They looked upon a lush, green field, with flowers sprinkled through the grass. At one end of the field was a huge white tent, decorated with rainbow bunting. And at the other was a tall pole, with loads of colourful ribbons hanging off it. In the middle of the field was a small bonfire, surrounded by wooden toadstools, logs and picnic tables. Strings of fairy lights were draped over the trees. Small candles flickered in lanterns. And everywhere they looked, animals with shiny fur and bright eyes were feasting, dancing, singing and laughing.

WINKLENUTS

'Holy moly!' said Ted, jumping up and down on the spot.

Rugs and beanbags were scattered under the branches of a large oak tree. Animals were lounging on them, snoozing or sipping drinks and having paw massages. Butterflies flapped around, telling each other jokes and laughing. It was *perfect*.

A hare in a wispy dress was standing on a small stage near the bonfire, playing the guitar. A crowd had gathered around her and were swaying their paws in the air as she sang.

'That's Anoushka Wispy,' sighed Sebastian Silver. 'She's *so* talented. We have concerts here every day, you know.'

'Wow!' gasped Ted and Willow.

'There's also an absolutely *darling* little theatre over the way,' said Sebastian. 'I suppose you have a theatre too?'

Ted and Willow looked at each other nervously.

'Um,' said Ted. '*Kind* of.'

'How long have you lot been here for?' barked Nancy.

'Oh, forever,' said Sebastian Silver. 'You'll find Twinklenuts Forest on maps from centuries ago.'

Nancy grunted.

'Grimwood not on any of these old maps, then?' she said.

Sebastian turned to look at Nancy properly. A strange smile danced around his lips. It looked sort of friendly, but also sort of not. Nancy was no fool. She had seen that kind of smile before.

'Not that I'm aware of,' he said. 'But I will double-check, young lady. I *honestly* thought it was just, you know, wasteland. Rubbish, filth and emptiness. I am SHOCKED to discover that it could be anybody's actual *home*.'

Nancy frowned.

Willow bounced between them and clutched the hem of Sebastian's smart jacket.

'Is there more?' she shrieked. 'Please show us more! I'm going out of my MIIIIIIIND!'

Sebastian laughed. 'Of course!' he said. 'You *must* see the Crystal Lake.'

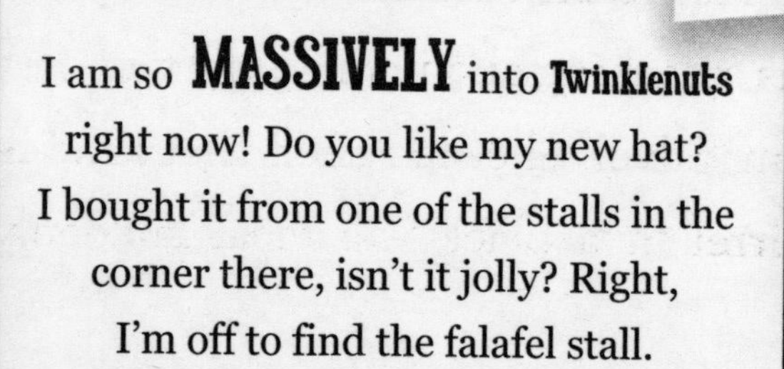

The light bounced off the perfectly flat surface of the Crystal Lake, making it sparkle and shimmer.

'It's why it's called the Crystal Lake,' said Sebastian Silver proudly. 'Isn't it fabulous?'

He dipped his paw into the clear, fresh water and raised some to his mouth.

'AAAAAH!' he said, smacking his lips together. 'Please, help yourselves. Drink, swim! It's all yours.'

Wiggy slurped up a big pawful. Then he waded into the water.

'Oooh, it's a delight!' he hooted.

'CANNONBAAAAAAAAAALL!' screamed Willow, landing with a massive splash.

Ted approached the lake more cautiously, but soon he was splashing about and giggling.

Sebastian Silver clicked his fingers twice and a squirrel in a black waistcoat suddenly appeared, holding a silver tray upon which balanced two cups.

'Coffee?' asked Sebastian Silver, handing a cup to Nancy. 'I have the beans flown in from Guatemala especially. You simply *must* try it.'

Nancy loved coffee, and this stuff smelled too good to resist. As she took her first sip, she heard a familiar cry.

'Treeeeeeebonk!'

She looked up and saw a squirrel fling itself headfirst into a tree trunk. It was wearing a very smart, professional-looking helmet.

'You play treebonk here as well?' she laughed. 'Wicked. Nice kit.'

Sebastian Silver gave a loud groan and rolled his eyes.

'Hiya, Chief!' said the treebonking squirrel, with a little wave.

'Hello, Reena,' nodded Sebastian wearily. He turned back to Nancy. 'Yes, I don't care much for treebonk myself, but it keeps the squirrels happy. They play it over in Grimsville, do they?'

Nancy nodded, taking another sip of coffee.

'You mean Grimwood,' she said. 'And yes, we do. I play a bit of it myself as it goes.'

Sebastian looked at her in surprise.

'A *fox*? Playing treebonk? How terribly . . . quaint. I honestly can't understand why *any*one would *want* to play treebonk. It's such a grubby, rough little game. There are *much* better things one could do with one's time.'

'Nah, it's brilliant,' said Nancy. 'And I'm pretty good at it.'

'Probably, probably,' said Sebastian. '*Actually*, they say that our Treebonk team is the finest Twinklenuts has ever produced. But – ha! – what would I know? I am but a humble fox.'

And he stretched himself out on a deckchair, his thick, shiny fur glinting in the sunshine.

Ted, Willow and Wiggy were still splashing about in the lake.

'Sis!' cried Ted. 'Come in and have a swim! It's so CLEAN you wouldn't believe it. No plastic bags or cans or weird foam . . . it's NOTHING like Grimwood.'

He dived underwater with a hoot.

'Nah, you're OK,' said Nancy, who had never been keen on water. Back in the Big City she used to get pushed into the river at night by gangs of delinquent geese. She shivered at the memory.

Ted swam to shore and scampered up the grassy bank, his fur dripping.

'Catch,' said Sebastian Silver, throwing him a thick, fluffy towel.

'Ooh, it feels like a soft cloud,' said Ted, drying his tail off. 'This place is just the best,

Mr S. Can I ask you a question?'

Sebastian Silver nodded, clearly charmed by Ted and his big, trusting eyes.

'How do you make your whiskers curl up at the end like that?' asked Ted.

'Oh, well, every respectable fox should use whisker wax, dear boy,' said Sebastian Silver.

'It looks so cool,' grinned Ted.

'You *do* comb your tail, don't you?' asked Sebastian Silver.

'Nah,' said Ted cheerfully. 'We just let them hang loose, don't we, Nancy?'

Nancy nodded.

'Goodness!' said Sebastian Silver. 'Whatever do your parents say? A young fox should always comb their tail. It's basic grooming!'

Ted rolled around on the towel to dry his back.

'Well, we don't have a mum and dad no more,' he said. 'Nancy looks after me.'

Sebastian Silver went quiet then. He looked over at Nancy, who coolly carried on sipping her coffee.

'Goodness me,' said Sebastian Silver. 'You poor thing. My father taught me everything there is to know about being a fox. Fishing, hunting, grooming, tailoring.'

'I teach him loads of stuff,' said Nancy flatly. But nobody heard her, because Ted was now sitting at Sebastian Silver's feet, wide-eyed in wonder.

'Cor, Mr S!' said Ted. 'I'd *love* to know all about that stuff! Could you teach me?'

Sebastian Silver chuckled. 'Well, for a start we should talk about that tatty old scarf you're wearing. Have you ever considered a neckerchief? We foxes always look *dashing* in a neckerchief.'

Ted giggled and clutched at his scarf, shyly.

'What a thoroughly charming fellow you are,' remarked Sebastian Silver. 'You remind me of me when I was a young fox. Such a *perfect* face, really. You'd fit right in.'

Nancy scowled. 'Fit in where?' she said. 'Here? No, thanks. We live in Grimwood, mate.'

Sebastian Silver sighed. 'Such a shame. We have so much to offer the right sort of animal in Twinklenuts. There's the fields, the lake, the theatre, the cinema, the library . . .'

'Cor, it all sounds amazing!' chirruped Willow, who had appeared wearing a fluffy dressing gown and sipping on a glass of fizzy orange. 'Just wait until I tell all my brothers and sisters!' Then she scratched her bottom and let out an enormous parp.

'Urgh,' sneered Nancy. 'You stink, Willow.'

'I do not!' snarled Willow. 'You stink!'

'Watch it, bunny,' growled Nancy.

'No, *you* watch it or I'll knock your block off!' shouted Willow.

Sebastian Silver's ears went flat and he narrowed his eyes.

'Um, my lovely guests,' he said in a low, quiet voice. 'In Twinklenuts we do not tolerate *anger* or *ruffian behaviours*. I do hope I've made myself clear.'

And he grinned so widely that sunbeams bounced off his teeth.

'Sorry, Mr Silver,' mumbled Willow, looking down and sheepishly grinding a foot into the grass.

Ted looked panicked.

'Yes, so sorry, Mr Silver! We're not *normally* so rude,' he said, glaring at Willow and Nancy.

'Maybe it's time we were going home,' said Nancy, giving Sebastian Silver a hard stare.

'Yes,' grinned Sebastian Silver. 'Maybe it is.'

Oh gosh, how awkward. Reminds me of when I got several of my feet stuck in the revolving door of a theatre once. Took ages to get me out, **red faces** all round.

10
11

CHAPTER SEVEN
Titus moans

Ted, Nancy, Willow and Wiggy bounced back from Twinklenuts and headed straight for Titus's caravan. The cheerful stag was sitting outside with Frank, working his way through an enormous plate of biscuits.

'We've discovered a new place!' shouted Willow. 'It's called Twinklenuts and it's amaaa aaaaaaaaaaaaaaaaaaaaaaaaaaaaaaaaaaaaaaaaaa aaaaaaaaaaaaaaaaaaaaaaaaaaaaaaaaaaaaaaaaaa aaaaaaaaaaaaaaaaaaaaaaaaaaaaaaaaaaaaaaaaaa aaaaaaaaaaaaaaaaaaaaaaaaaaaaaaaazing!'

'And, and there was a LAKE and a theatre and all sorts of brilliant things!' said Ted, hopping up and down. 'It was SO perfect and pretty, Titus! AND we got free fizzy orange! But then Willow farted and we had to leave.'

Titus opened his mouth in shock and half a biscuit fell out.

'Yeah, there's a mayor too,' said Nancy. 'A fox. Some dude called Sebastian Silver. Posh fella. Not sure what his game is.'

'He's SO cool!' said Ted, eyes shining. 'A proper grown-up fox, Titus!'

'Basically,' continued Willow, 'Twinklenuts is just like Grimwood, but REALLY clean and fun and about a hundred times better in every way.'

Wiggy noticed that Titus suddenly looked very sad and had stopped eating his biscuits.

'Did you say . . . that there's another

mayor?' whispered Titus.

'Oh, he's just some silly old fox,' said Wiggy gently, resting his large badgery paw on Titus's shoulder. 'Well . . . a dashing old fox with twinkly eyes, glossy fur and a fantastic jacket. But an old fox all the same.'

A fat tear rolled down Titus's face.

'What's up with him?' asked Nancy.

Then Titus threw his plate of biscuits to the floor and sobbed loudly into his hooves.

Frank shook his head.

'You know how sensitive he is!' he said. 'You had no business going anywhere.' He draped a large owlish wing around Titus.

'I've always been scared of this,' howled Titus. 'Of there being a NEW place. An exciting new place everyone loves so much that they leave Grimwood for ever and I am left all aloooooooone!'

And he sobbed so much that his tears drowned Dame Evelyn Taylor, a small fly who had been sitting on the table minding her own business.

Willow clambered up onto Titus's lap and shoved her paws deep into his gigantic nostrils to try to stop the flow of snot.

'We'd never leave you, Titus. And we'd never leave Grimwood either,' she said. 'It's home! Even though they *did* have free hot dogs.'

Suddenly, a low rumbling sound made the ground shudder and shake.

'HONK, HONK! COMING THROUGH!

Make way, losers, make way!'

It was the badgers' Jeep, being driven by Wiggy's big brother, Monty. In the back sat his three other brothers, who were all called Jeremy. The Jeep skidded to a stop right in front of Wiggy.

'Oh, hey, bro,' said Monty.

Wiggy looked confused.

'Where are you all going?' he asked.

Monty adjusted his wraparound sunglasses.

'Twinklenuts, pal,' he said. 'You heard of it? There's a rumour going around that it's totally top-notch! Word is there's a massive lake, tennis courts, free fizzy orange, a posho restaurant . . .'

'Yes, I, um, I've actually just been there,' said Wiggy. 'Were you just going to leave without telling me?'

Monty shrugged.

'Sorry, old chap, we just didn't really think about you,' he said, checking his fur in the Jeep's mirror. 'Maybe you should stay here with your weirdo pals. Seems more your kinda place, don't you think?'

'Oh,' said Wiggy and he looked down at his feet.

'Bye, Wiggster,' said Jeremy.

'See you later, bro,' said Jeremy 2.

'You can totes have my bunk bed,' said little Jeremy 3, who was the nicest Jeremy.

'Yah boo sucks, Wiggster!' hooted Monty. 'Don't be a loser all your life.'

And they drove away, leaving Wiggy behind.

Nancy nudged him.

Oh NO! How horrid.

'Yo,' she said. 'You all right, dude?'

Wiggy nodded and wiped his eyes on his tatty old school tie.

Titus sighed.

'I knew it – it's starting!' he said. 'The badgers have left Grimwood. Who will be next?'

'Absolute HOODLUMS!' quacked Ingrid, who had been napping on the caravan roof. 'Grimwood is better off without them.'

'I know!' said Willow brightly. 'Let's make Grimwood all POSH and EXCITING and GLAMOROUS and then everyone will want to stay here! Cos at the moment it's smelly and grubby and looks like a massive bin.'

Titus scratched his snout.

'You could be onto something there, young rabbit,' he said. 'OK, nobody move. I'll be back soon!'

And he zoomed really fast down the hill yelling **'Wheeeeeeeeeee!'**, which is what you have to do if you ever go really fast down a hill.

Everyone waited and waited and waited.

They waited *so* long that Ted wrote a poem, Willow assembled the world's longest daisy chain and a wasp called Igor died of boredom. Several hours later, Titus clambered back up the hill with a flip chart and a pointy stick.

'My dears! I have some exciting plans for Grimwood's future!' he trilled. He pointed to a sheet of paper on the flip chart which read:

'NEXT,' shouted Frank.

PLAN NUMBER TWO:

Grimwood Aquarium!

We invite some deadly sharks, a giant octopus and some killer whales to come and live in Grimwood. However, we would also need to find loads of fish tanks and quite a bit of water.

'NEXT,' shouted everyone.

PLAN NUMBER THREE:

We smear honey and glue over absolutely everything, so that whenever anyone visits they get stuck and cannot leave.

'I like it!' said Willow.

Frank flew over to Titus and held his hoof.

'I don't think any of these plans will work, chief,' he said gently.

Titus kicked over the flip chart and sighed. Then he slapped his knees.

'Right, that's it. I'm going to pop over to Twinklenuts right now. They are our neighbours, so it's important that I am friendly and introduce myself. After all, it's the Grimwood way!'

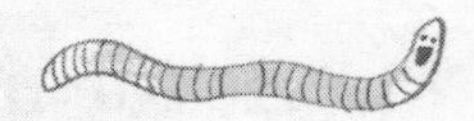

Everyone boinged their way across the mattresses on the Swamp of Despair, except Frank who swooped low over their heads. As the gang neared the edge of the swamp, they heard a low hoot from Frank, and he pointed one wing towards something looming up ahead of them. It was a high fence, made from a tangle of metal and wood, with nasty-looking barbed wire curled on top. Ted was confused. He was certain the fence hadn't been there earlier. He ran over to it and saw a sign. It said:

'Woah!' said Willow. 'That is the rudest thing I have ever seen. Well, whatever. I can climb that thing in five seconds flat.'

She grabbed onto the fence with both paws.

ZZZZZZZZZAAAAAAPPPPPP!

She flew high into the air.

'Willow!' cried Ted.

Smoke and the smell of singed fur wafted around the fence.

Ted bounced his way back until he found Willow face down on one of the mattresses.

'HOW RUDE,' said a lightly electrocuted Willow. 'I'm going to give that Sebastian Whatsit a massive smack on the nose for that.'

'Hmm. Not very neighbourly, is it?' frowned Nancy, gazing up at the horrible electric fence.

'I'm *sure* there's been a mistake,' said Ted. 'Sebastian Silver was SO friendly to us. I bet he'll be really annoyed when he finds out someone's put this horrible fence up!'

Nancy raised her eyebrows and looked at Titus. It was a look that said: 'Something weird is going on here but I don't wanna freak out Ted'.

So Titus just patted Ted gently on the head and said, 'You're probably right, little chap. I'll try to meet with him another time. Let's go home.'

THE GREAT GRIMWOOD EGG CHALLENGE!

****

Who can eat the biggest pile of eggs?

Let's find out!

Frank: 36 eggs

Nancy: 50 eggs

Ingrid: 'How very dare you!'

Wiggy: 390 eggs

Titus: 2 eggs ('On toasted brioche with some grated truffle, please')

Ted: 15 eggs

Eggbert Eggbertson, the Famous Egg-Eating Horse of Amsterdam: 34,565 eggs

Well, that was a bit of a **one-horse** race, wasn't it?

CHAPTER EIGHT
Sebastian Silver's Great Big Plan

In the clearing outside Titus's caravan, there were logs to be sat upon and tables on which to rest paws and cups of tea. It was usually a cheery place, but this morning the vibe was gloomy. Titus plonked a teapot down and sighed. He was eating a big bowl of

PUNISHMENT MUESLI.

'Ooh, yum,' said Frank, swooping down to sit beside him. 'Punishment Muesli, my favourite!'

Titus grunted. Punishment Muesli was the most horrible breakfast ever, and he only ate it when he felt sad, because it made him feel sadder, and sometimes that felt like the right thing to do.

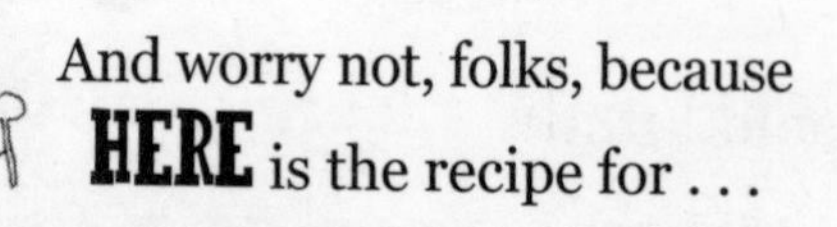

PUNISHMENT MUESLI

INGREDIENTS:

3 twigs, snapped into tiny little pieces
½ spoonful of grit
10 small pebbles
5 leaves
1 small onion, which is old and soft and has grown weird long knobbly bits
2 empty snail shells, to garnish

METHOD:

Put all of the ingredients into a bowl.
Point at the bowl and tell it off for being disgusting.
Add milk. Enjoy!

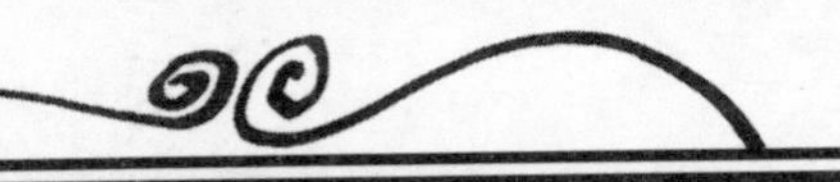

Hello! Eric **'Health and Safety' Dynamite** here to ask you NOT to make or eat Punishment Muesli because it will taste horrible and you may die, which would be a total downer. Thaaaaaanks!

'I have a feeling of doom and dread, Frank,' said Titus. 'Doom and dread!'

'Ach, don't get yourself all wound up, Titus,' said Frank.

'Yes, you are making a big Titus-shaped fuss about nothing,' announced Ingrid, waddling out of the caravan with a chilled tomato juice and a dish of olives. 'So we have some neighbours. So what? So their place is nicer. So what? So they've put up an electric fence to keep us out. Who cares? Not me. I do not give any of the monkeys.'

And she tossed an olive into her beak.

Suddenly, the sky went dark and a loud noise gave the friends a jolt.

CHOP-CHOP-CHOP-CHOP-CHOP . . .

Everyone ducked under the table as a strong wind blew dust and leaves into the air.

When they opened their eyes, they saw a tall, handsome figure with glossy fur and a thick, luxurious tail stepping out of a shiny silver helicopter.

'It's him,' croaked Titus.

Sebastian Silver strode towards the caravan. Behind him scurried a stoat, carrying rolls of paper that it kept almost dropping. And behind

the stoat was a serious-looking hare, holding a red briefcase.

'Titus!' boomed Sebastian Silver. 'It is Titus, isn't it?'

Titus picked himself up off the ground, dusted himself down and nodded.

'Hello! I'm Sebastian Silver. Perhaps some of your . . . *friends* have mentioned me?'

Even though he was in shock, Titus was an extremely polite stag. He took a deep breath.

'Titus Crazyhorns at your service! I welcome you and your friends to Grimwood.'

And he did an awkward bow.

'Lovely!' beamed Sebastian Silver. 'I wonder if you have time for a little chat?'

'Bananas!' screamed Titus. 'Er, sorry, I mean, yes, of course.'

Sebastian raised his eyebrows and shoved the stoat forwards.

'This is my associate, Susan Kidneys,' said Sebastian. The stoat took a bow, immediately dropping all the rolls of paper.

'And this is my lawyer, Fatima Hostile,' he continued. The hare gave a quick, stern nod.

'Anyone for an iced bun?' asked Titus weakly.

'No, thank you. We're here on important business, Mr Crazyhorns,' said Sebastian Silver, sitting himself down without asking. He nodded at Susan Kidneys. The stoat spread out one roll of paper on the table, placing pebbles in the corners so it stayed flat.

'Golly,' said Titus. 'What's this?'

'A map that has been sitting in the Twinklenuts library for years,' said Sebastian Silver grandly. 'After I learned about Grimwood, I did some digging around and just happened to find it. Aren't we lucky?'

Titus leant forward to get a closer look but

was whacked on the snout with a ruler.

'You have NOT been authorized to look at the map,' said Fatima Hostile, who was the ruler-whacker.

'Now what we have here,' said Sebastian Silver, 'is a map of Twinklenuts. And, I suppose, of Grimwood. You see, the border of Twinklenuts is *here*.'

Susan Kidneys traced a huge circle over most of the map.

'You may now look at the map,' said Fatima Hostile.

Titus frowned.

'So where is Grimwood?' he asked. 'Is it that little red blob over there?'

Sebastian Silver peered closely. 'Ah, no, that's a splodge of raspberry jam from my breakfast scone,' he said.

Susan traced a *much* smaller circle with her

stick. 'You see this area here, yes?'

'The one that says "barren wasteland"?' asked Titus.

'Indeed,' said Susan, pushing her glasses up her nose. 'The area you call "Grimwood" is actually this patch of dirty useless land INSIDE the border of Twinklenuts Forest.'

Titus frowned.

'I . . . I don't understand,' he muttered.

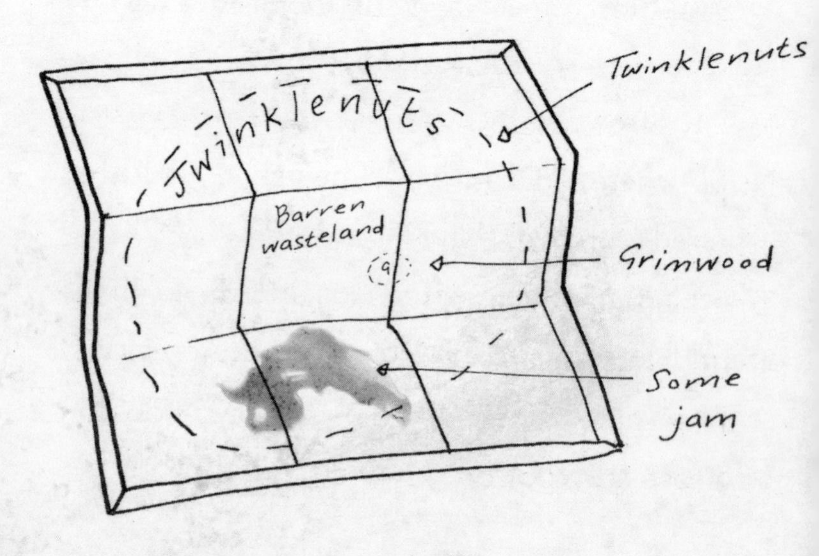

'It means, old chap, that Grimwood doesn't exist!' hooted Sebastian Silver. He stretched his arms out. 'This - all of this - belongs to Twinklenuts! *You* belong to Twinklenuts!'

Then he threw back his head and laughed.

Frank perched on Titus's antlers.

'Look here, sonny,' he said to Sebastian Silver. 'We tried to visit you lot and got zapped by your electric fence. That wasn't very neighbourly now, was it? So, I suggest you buzz off, pronto.'

Sebastian Silver waved his paw at Frank.

'Oh, there's no need for any bad feelings, Mr Owl! And I'm SO sorry about the fence. But lately we've had a rabble of err . . . *guests* from elsewhere and, well, I can't let just *anyone* into Twinklenuts now, can I? Fatima, show him the Twinklenuts Charter.'

The hare opened her important-looking briefcase and took out a glossy sheet of card.

THE TWINKLENUTS CHARTER

Animals who live in Twinklenuts must NOT:

1. Have moustaches
2. Be sad, miserable or upset EVER
3. Have snotty noses
4. Parp or burp
5. Have a wonky face

Animals who live in Twinklenuts MUST:

1. Look totally fantastic and smile AT ALL TIMES
2. Speak at least three languages
3. Smell delightful AT ALL TIMES
4. Be great at maths AND spelling
5. Be able to draw a perfect circle with absolutely no wobbles

(Failure to meet any of the above guidelines will result in your immediate imprisonment, unless we are in a really good mood. Thaaaaaaaaaaaanks! ☺)

'Hmph!' quacked Ingrid. 'Ridiculous! These conditions are entirely nonsense!'

'I'm afraid it is illegal to say that,' said Fatima Hostile. She took some handcuffs out of her briefcase. 'I am placing you under arrest.'

Sebastian Silver chuckled.

'Now, now, Fatima,' he said. 'Let's be kind.'

Fatima glared at the glamorous duck, but slowly put the handcuffs down.

Meanwhile, Ted and Willow had wandered over to Titus's caravan for tea and chats. Ted gasped when he saw the elegant swish of Sebastian Silver's tail.

'Mr Silver, hello, Mr Silver!' yelped Ted, running over to him.

'Ah, the charming younglings!' said Sebastian Silver. 'Why, Ted. May I just say your fur is looking *fantastic* today.'

Ted giggled and blushed.

'Oh, children,' said Titus, staggering backwards into a rusty old deckchair. 'Our new neighbour Sebastian Silver has discovered something quite terrible!'

Sebastian Silver leant over and clutched Titus's hoof.

'There, there, old chap,' he purred. 'It's not a *disaster*, is it?'

'What's happened?' asked Ted, his tail drooping.

'It's actually FANTASTIC news,' said Sebastian Silver. 'This,' he said, waving around at Grimwood, '*all* this . . . is going to become part of Twinklenuts Forest!'

Ted and Willow gasped and looked at Titus, who nodded sadly.

'Y . . . yes. He appears to have found some kind of *map*,' he said weakly. 'Which means Grimwood will be no more.'

'And that's not all,' grinned Sebastian Silver. 'Now that the Magic Tower will belong to me – er, I mean, Twinklenuts, I'll have enough electricity to finally build THIS!'

He nodded at Susan Kidneys, who spread out *another* huge sheet of paper . . .

SILVERTOWN
HOLIDAY PARK
Flashing lights!
Meet the REAL Sebastian Silver!
Food and things!
Amazing rides!
Trees trees trees!
Kittens!
Where all your dreams come true!*
*NB Does not include ALL dreams, especially not ones about winning the lottery, going to school naked, growing a tail, becoming Prime Minister, fighting a massive dragon, your gran becoming a dolphin, or that one about losing your pencil case and then finding it under a hedge.

'Woaaaaaaah,' said Willow. 'Look at the size of those rollercoasters!'

'Wow!' said Ted. 'This place looks amazing!'

Sebastian Silver beamed.

'Oh, I'd *hoped* you'd like it,' he said. 'It really will be quite the money-spinner. Visitors will come from miles around. It will be the most exciting place on Earth! They'll ride the rides, buy the merch, take pics of all of us looking *a-ma-zing*, and I'll become a squillionaire!'

Fatima Hostile coughed.

'Sorry, I mean *we* will become squillionaires,' grinned Sebastian Silver, gesturing at everyone. 'And now that we can build over Grimwood, there'll be *plenty* of room for all the other bits and pieces.'

'What "bits and pieces"?' grizzled Frank.

'Oh, you know,' said Sebastian, waving his paw airily. 'Boring stuff. Roads. Shiny skyscrapers.

A multi-storey car park. A massive statue of me.'

'Um, and where exactly will all of that go?' asked Titus nervously.

'Well,' said Sebastian, stroking his whiskers thoughtfully, 'we're actually standing in the very spot where the multi-storey car park will be built, isn't that right, Susan?'

Susan nodded. She was wandering around, very seriously measuring the ground and trees. Every now and then she would stop and jot numbers down in a small notebook.

Just then there was a low growl.

Everyone turned to see Nancy. She was glaring at Sebastian Silver. He pretended to ignore her.

'Anyway, Titus, the other thing is you won't be Mayor of Grimwood any more,' continued the fox. 'But is that *really* so bad? You deserve a rest. So just sign these papers and it'll all be done and dusted.'

Fatima clicked open her briefcase and took out a stack of paper.

'What exactly am I signing?' asked Titus.

'Oh, a very dull contract,' said Sebastian. 'It just says that Grimwood will become Twinklenuts, I'll become mayor of *everywhere* and I will own everything, blah, blah, blah. Boring, boring, boring!'

Titus gasped.

Frank hooted.

Willow growled.

Ted whimpered.

Ingrid laid an egg.

And Nancy marched straight over to Fatima Hostile, grabbed the papers and ate them.

'Nancy!' cried Ted.

Sebastian Silver smiled at Nancy, but his eyes flashed with fury.

'Nah, we ain't signing nuffink,' said Nancy, scraps of paper scattered around her feet. 'You can't make us.'

Sebastian Silver folded his arms and narrowed his eyes.

'Mr Silver,' said Titus. 'Grimwood is our home. I love every animal who lives here. I cannot just . . . sign it all away.'

Sebastian Silver nodded.

'I understand, old stag,' he said, his voice sounding less friendly than before. 'But the map clearly shows us that *everything* belongs to me.'

'So, what happens to us when you flatten Grimwood with your stupid theme park?' growled Nancy.

Sebastian Silver chuckled.

'Oh, don't worry, you feisty little thing,' he said. 'There will be *plenty* of space for everyone.'

But Nancy wasn't having it.

'Oh yeah? What about when we don't measure up to your stupid rules? You going to chuck us all in jail, are you?'

Nancy snatched the Twinklenuts Charter from Fatima Hostile.

'It's a load of rubbish,' she snarled. 'None of us are gonna "smile at all times" or "look fantastic at all times" or "speak at least three languages".'

'Yes, and the bit about drawing a circle worried me,' said Titus. 'I'm not a natural artist.'

Sebastian Silver held a clenched paw to his forehead.

'Well, maybe you'll have to go and live SOMEWHERE ELSE then!' he shouted, his eyes suddenly flashing with rage.

Ted's lip wobbled.

'Please don't shout at us, Mr Silver,' he said quietly.

'Oh, young Ted,' smiled Sebastian Silver, reaching over to ruffle his fur. '*You* mustn't worry. I can see a bright future for you in Twinklenuts, dear boy! Why, you could even be my little sidekick! You'd like that, wouldn't you?'

Nancy walked over and thwacked Sebastian Silver's paw away from Ted's head.

'Now listen. You can't just swoosh in here and take Grimwood,' said Nancy. 'I don't like bullies. And you, pal, are a bully.'

Sebastian growled a low, deep growl.

'I can do whatever I want,' he hissed. 'In fact, I could kick you all out right now, if I felt like it.'

Everyone gasped.

'You wouldn't *really* do that to us, would you, Mr Silver?' whimpered Ted. He had thought Sebastian Silver was cool and ace and seeing him be a nasty rotter was hurting Ted's head.

Nancy's mind was racing. She *had* to save Grimwood, and everyone in it. Her brain whizzed and whirred and wongled. In the distance, she heard a faint squawk, and then a small explosion. It was just Pamela and Sharon doing some experiments up in the Magic Tower.

And THAT's when she had a brilliant idea.

It would be tricky. But it was the only thing she could think of.

'OK, Silver,' she said. 'You want the Magic Tower, do ya?'

Sebastian examined his claws and yawned.

'Yeah, like, OBVS,' he sighed.

'Then you've got a problem,' smirked Nancy. She looked at Frank and winked. 'And she's a very BIG problem. Frank, can you call Pamela, please?'

Frank held his treebonk whistle to his beak.

He blew it loudly, three times.

'What on earth . . .' said Sebastian.

There was a very loud **PCKAAAAAW**.

Fatima Hostile and Susan Kidneys squealed at the same time and dashed under Titus's caravan.

'What on earth is the matter with you?' finished Sebastian Silver.

Pamela swooped down grandly from the clouds.

'What do you want, Frank?' she yelled. 'I am very busy exploding things! **PCKAAAW**.'

Then Pamela spotted Sebastian Silver.

'Who the heck are YOU?' she asked. 'Do you want to be on my radio show? Today's topics are: Are chocolate bars getting smaller?

Should we let babies get tattoos? Are *all* lemurs untrustworthy?'

Sebastian Silver looked confused.

'We was just tellin' him about the Magic Tower, Pamela,' said Nancy casually.

Pamela's eyes turned into giant saucers. She started squawking very loudly.

'NOBODY IS ALLOWED NEAR MY TOWER UNLESS I SAY SO!' she shrieked. 'NOT THE WORMS OR THE BIRDS OR THE MOOSES OR THE ALIENS OR THE TEENY TINY ANTS RIDING IN A TEENY TINY ANT BUS OR THE HORSES OR THE COWS OR THE COWS DRESSED UP AS HORSES OR THE–'

Frank blew his whistle again.

'Easy, Pamela, easy,' he hooted, until she settled down.

Sebastian, meanwhile, looked *most* alarmed.

'And what do you *do* to strangers who get

too close to the Magic Tower, Pamela?' asked Nancy grinning.

This time, Pamela's eyes narrowed into tiny slits. She ruffled her feathers, spread out her gigantic wings and started bouncing from one foot to the other.

'I BITE OFF THEIR HEADS AND SQUISH UP THEIR BODIES AND USE THEIR BONES AS MARACAS!' she screamed.

'Thought so,' said Frank. 'We just wanted to check. Thanks, Pamela.'

'Adios!' said Pamela. **'PCKAAAAAAW!'**

She saluted Titus then launched into the air.

Ted glanced at Sebastian Silver. 'She's the one I told you about when we first met,' he said, in a small voice.

'Ah yes,' said Titus. 'Even if I *was* to sign Grimwood over to you today, Pamela would probably kill you pretty quickly. She hates strangers going near the Magic Tower.'

Sebastian Silver growled.

'Unless . . .' said Nancy.

'Unless WHAT?' snapped Sebastian Silver, furious his plan was being fiddled with.

'Unless we tell her not to,' said Nancy. 'Pamela listens to us. If we say so, she *probably* won't eat you.'

'Fine,' he snarled. 'What will it take?'

Nancy's eyes flickered to the others. She took a deep breath.

'Treebonk,' she said.

'Urgh,' shivered Sebastian. 'Dreadful game. What about it?'

'We'll have a treebonk match,' said Nancy. 'Grimwood vs. Twinklenuts. If we win, you leave us alone. If you win, you'll get Grimwood, the Magic Tower and we'll tell Pamela not to murder you.'

'OOOOOOOOH!' said everyone.

Frank waggled his eyebrows in alarm.

Sebastian Silver thought for a bit. And then he started to laugh.

'We have the finest Treebonk team in the land!' he hooted. 'We'll beat you with our eyes closed. It won't be a fair fight at all. OK, it's a deal!'

He held out his paw to Titus, ready to shake on it.

Titus looked at Nancy with big, worried eyes. But Nancy looked determined. They would practise like mad and do everything they could to beat Twinklenuts. She nodded at Titus.

Titus slowly reached over and shook Sebastian Silver's paw.

'D-d-deal,' he stammered.

'HA! Excellent,' grinned Sebastian Silver. 'My people will be in touch with your people.

Jolly good! Well, we'll be on our way.'

And as he left, Sebastian Silver swooshed his tail so powerfully it kicked clouds of dust into the air, making everyone splutter and cough.

'My dear, brave Nancy,' said Titus. 'How are we going to beat them?'

'Don't worry,' she said with a grin. 'I've got a plan.'

'Oh, thank goodness!' said Titus. 'I knew you would.'

Ted watched his sister. She was quietly chewing her paws. And that's when he knew that Nancy didn't have a plan at all.

CHAPTER NINE
Operation: Twinklenuts

Nancy woke up and saw that, as usual, Ted had left a mug of coffee by her bedside. She slurped it gratefully. He was a good cub, she thought to herself. Before she went outside, she stopped for a moment. She pulled back the tatty old blanket that was hanging on the wall.

There were two paw prints, pressed into the mud.

Her paw fitted neatly in the smaller one.

Nancy sighed. She had found the prints not long after they had arrived in Grimwood. She knew it sounded weird, but part of her had wondered if they had been made by their mum and dad. Even though, as far as she knew, her parents had never been to Grimwood – so it was just a silly daydream, really. She didn't tell Ted about them. He'd just get all excited, and what was the point of that? The paw prints probably meant nothing at all.

'Just forget about it,' Nancy growled to herself. She downed the coffee and headed for treebonk practice.

Frank swooped up and down the line of squirrels. He hadn't slept a wink after yesterday's visit from Sebastian Silver and his furry associates.

'Now listen here, team,' said Frank, puffing

out his owly chest. 'We've got quite the treebonk battle ahead of us. But we're strong, and fast, and with practice, we can get stronger and faster. Because we're not just playing to win. We're playing for our HOME. We're playing to SAVE GRIMWOOD!'

Frank waited for everyone to whoop and cheer.

But there was silence. He turned around and saw that everyone was huddled around a squirrel called Martin who was showing off his new light-up trainers.

'WILL YOU PLEASE PAY ATTENTION, TEAM?' Frank shouted, so loudly that everyone jumped (and a *tiny* bit of wee came out of Martin).

'What's the plan then, kid?' said Frank to Nancy, after he'd sent the squirrels out to run some laps.

'I'm not sure yet,' said Nancy. 'But I'm working on it.'

Ted and Willow were sitting on top of a mossy rock, sharing a bag of sweets.

'Green one, please,' said Frank, holding out a talon.

'Urgh! Only weirdos like the green ones,' said Willow, handing over a sweet. 'Frank, I don't mean to be a downer, but you guys are never gonna beat Twinklenuts. Grimwood is toast!'

Frank sighed. He knew Willow was probably right.

'We need to know more about their team,' said Nancy. 'Learn about their strengths. Find a weak spot.'

'Frank! Why don't you fly over there and take a look?' said Ted.

Frank shook his head.

'Sebastian Silver's no fool,' he said. 'He'll have lookouts waiting for me to swoop over and spy on them. I'll get shot down by a catapult.'

Willow started hopping up and down on the spot.

'I know, I know, I know, I know!' she cried.

'What do you know?' said Frank.

'We need a SPY,' said Willow.

'The problem with spies,' said Nancy, 'is that if they are a good spy, you will never know they are a spy. But if you know that someone is a spy, then they are not a very good spy.'

'OK, misery-pants, then what about someone

that used to be a spy? An EX-spy?' said Willow.

'Guess that might work,' grunted Nancy. 'But who do we know that used to be a spy?'

Willow grinned.

'Back in a mo!' she hooted, and she bounced into the woods, leaving Ted chewing thoughtfully on a fizzy cola bottle.

Ten minutes later…

'QUAAAAAAAAAAAAAACK!' quacked Ingrid. She had been having a lovely nap and refused to move from her comfy island of shopping trolleys. So Willow had just lifted her *and* a shopping trolley out of the Small Pond and wheeled them through the woods. Ingrid had complained loudly the whole way.

'The duck?' scoffed Nancy. 'What's she gonna do?'

Ingrid narrowed her eyes.

'Before I was a wildly successful business-duck, I was an AC-TOR,' she hissed.

'Yes, yes, we all know,' moaned Nancy.

'And before I was an AC-TOR I was . . . I was a top-secret SPY,' said Ingrid, folding her wings and looking very pleased with herself.

'Nah,' said Nancy. 'I don't believe it.'

Ingrid adjusted her turban and slowly clambered out of the shopping trolley. She wandered over to Nancy.

'Say that again,' said Ingrid quietly.

'I said I don't believe that *you* were ever a spy,' shrugged Nancy. 'With those soft feathers and earrings and that posho hat? Ha! As if.'

There was a scuffle, a quack and lots of dust. A few seconds later, Nancy was on the ground, her arms twisted behind her back. Ingrid was sitting on her head, reapplying her lipstick.

'I *was* a spy,' said Ingrid, snapping her small mirror shut.

'Woaaaah!' said Ted. 'You totally flattened Nancy. That's so cool!'

'Now, how can I be of service?' asked Ingrid.

'We need you to sneak into Twinklenuts,' said Frank. 'We need to know what their treebonk game is like. Who's on the team, how they play, what their tricks are.'

Ingrid nodded.

'This is no problem,' she said.

‘I’m coming with you,’ said Nancy. ‘I wanna check out their moves.’

‘And me and Willow too!’ said Ted. ‘We’ll be a cool little Grimwood gang.’

‘Nah,’ said Nancy. ‘You ain’t coming, squirt. You and your bunny pal can stay put.’

‘Oh, pleeeeeeeeeeeeease!’ whined Ted.

‘Don’t worry, Ted,’ smirked Willow. ‘She needs us. We’re small and can get into tight spaces AND we’re brilliant at being lookouts AND we both like cheese AND my favourite colour is orange AND I won’t stop talking until she lets us come AND . . .’

‘OK, OK, I give up,’ groaned Nancy.

‘Can *I* come?’ asked Felipe, a passing bumblebee.

‘NO,’ said everyone, because it was obvious that Felipe would be a total nightmare.

'What about the electric fence?' said Willow. 'I ain't burning my paws again!'

'Now listen,' said Ingrid. 'If you are all going to be top-secret spies like me, you need to start acting like it. No moaning. No loud noises. No disco dancing. We go under cover of darkness. Meet me by the Magic Tower at midnight.'

You could still just about see the Magic Tower at night thanks to the huge number of gadgets in Pamela the eagle's nest. She had been having a fantastic time with her new best friend, Sharon the Party Crow.

Sharon was in awe of Pamela's collection of mobile phones, wires, televisions, radios and other contraptions.

'You could do a loooooot of damage with this stuff,' she'd said, giving a low whistle.

'I know!' said a delighted Pamela. 'Let us do much damage.'

'Ooh, have you ever thought about making a glitter cannon?' asked Sharon.

'Does it explode?' asked Pamela.

'Yes,' said Sharon.

'Then yes! Let us make the biggest glitter cannon the world has ever seen!'

While the two daredevil birds were a-chittin' and a-chattin' about glitter cannons, Nancy, Ted and Willow stood at the base of the Magic Tower, waiting for Ingrid.

'She's late,' huffed Willow, chomping on a Cosmic Knobbler.

But then the ground beneath their paws rumbled and shook.

'WUUUARGH!' yelled Ted, hopping backwards as a hole appeared in the ground.

Out popped the snout of Emo Omar, who was a mole and also an 'underground poet'.

'All right, Omar,' said Willow, chucking him a Cosmic Knobbler. 'What you doing?'

'He's with me,' came a familiar voice, and then Ingrid clambered out of the hole. She shook the soil from her feathers and gave a quack. 'Our mole friend here is going to tunnel us into Twinklenuts.'

Emo Omar gave a little bow.

'I have written a poem for the occasion,' he said.

Nancy slapped her forehead in despair.

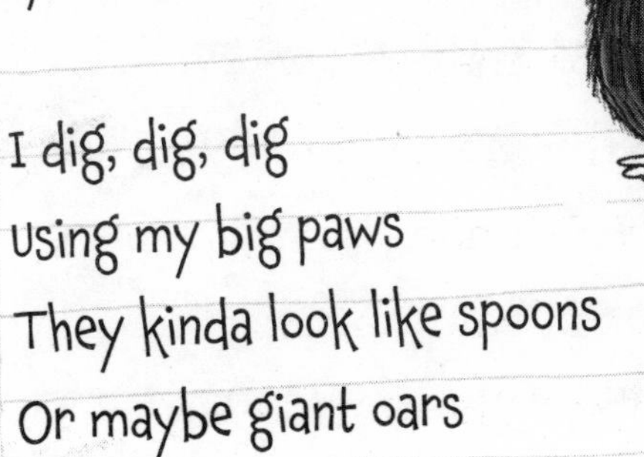

Digging for Victory

By Emo Omar

I dig, dig, dig
Using my big paws
They kinda look like spoons
Or maybe giant oars

I dig to save my home
From that stupid posho fox
Underground I roam
Ignoring nasty rocks

On my own it won't be easy
So these dudes will help me dig
These other moles are friends of mine
Akbar, Flo and Stig.
(FIN)

And three other moles plopped out of the hole and gave a little bow.

'Amazing!' applauded Willow. 'You guys are *the best* at digging. When do we go?'

Ingrid looked at her watch, which was weird because she wasn't wearing one, so really she just looked at her wing.

'Riiiiiiiiight about . . . NOW,' she said.

CHAPTER TEN
The library

The moles tunnelled through the night, being careful not to hit the Twinklenuts electric fence. Ingrid glanced at her extremely

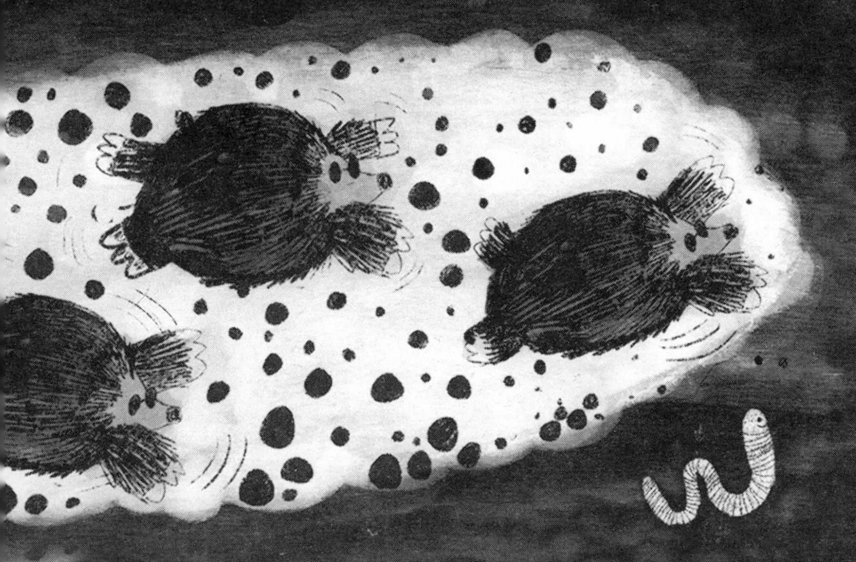

hi-tech satellite navigation system, which she had borrowed from Pamela. It seemed to be held together with rubber bands and old chewing gum but Pamela insisted that it worked 'just fine'.

'We are in Twinklenuts,' Ingrid announced grandly. 'So now we must dig upwards. Dig, I tell you!' She thumped a mole with her handbag to hurry them up.

Emo Omar was the first to emerge, and he immediately put on his sunglasses as his sensitive mole eyes adjusted to the bright light.

They were in a huge, musty room. The wooden floor was covered in tatty rugs and there were rows and rows of small tables. In front of every table were a lamp and a brown leather chair. And surrounding the tables were oodles of bookshelves, totally crammed with books.

'There's a special word for this kind of place,' gasped Willow.

'Yes. It's called a library,' said Nancy.

'Something like... the bookyplace,' said Willow, ignoring Nancy entirely. 'The lonkywonk . . . the wordybank . . .'

'I said it's called a library,' said Nancy.

'The fustyroom . . . the bonkenhause . . . the wonkywang . . .'

'LIBRARY,' said Nancy, shoving Willow to one side and marching into the room.

Emo Omar scurried straight for the poetry section. The other moles scattered, keen to explore.

There was a huge door leading off from the main library room. Nancy pushed it open and was faced with a maze of corridors. She gave a low whistle. 'How big *is* this place?' she wondered aloud as she stepped through the door and continued on.

Every now and then she would pass a large, locked door. She tried every single one, but none of them opened. Nancy grunted in frustration. They needed to find a way *out* of the library if they were ever going to spy on the Twinklenuts treebonk team.

Nancy was about to turn back when she spotted what looked like a trapdoor. She bent down and pressed her ear to it. Could she hear voices? She couldn't be sure.

Meanwhile, Ted was roaming around between the bookshelves, pulling out books here and there. There was a whole section dedicated to a newsletter called *The Twinklenuts Telegraph*. He took one out at random and gasped at the headline:

The Twinklenuts Telegraph.

NEW MAYOR FOR TWINKLENUTS

In a shock result, mysterious newcomer Sebastian Silver has been elected as Mayor of Twinklenuts by 154 votes! The old mayor, Crusty McTavish, has left office with immediate effect. Most residents of Twinklenuts are 'stunned' and 'surprised' as Crusty McTavish had been a popular and kind mayor for many years.

'I've got BIG plans for Twinklenuts,' said Sebastian Silver. 'Crusty McTavish allowed the townsfolk of Twinklenuts to get smelly, lazy and ugly. But things are going to change around here. I'm going to clean this place up. Hotels! Roads! Funfairs! Shopping malls! A space station! Trust me, soon the money's going to start rollin' in and we're all going to be RICH, RICH beyond our wildest dreams!'

Crusty McTavish was not available for comment, and a nearby worm advised that he has 'gone on a very long cruise in Antarctica to look at penguins'.

'Cor,' said Ted. 'Sebastian must be SO clever to become mayor just like that,' he said. 'And he looks *so* cool. I wonder if all grown-up foxes dress so well.'

Willow had hopped over and rolled her eyes.

'Sebastian this, Sebastian that,' she snapped. 'Have you forgotten that rotter wants to take Grimwood away from us?'

'Of course not,' said Ted. 'But to be fair, according to that map, Grimwood is already *in* Twinklenuts.'

Willow narrowed her eyes.

'Hmph! I think it's a stupid map. And what about Titus? I don't trust this Sebastian Silver as far as I could throw him,' said the cute little bunny-wunny. 'And I bet I could throw him *really* far.'

Ingrid the duck had hopped up to the very top of the bookshelves and was tapping the ceiling.

'What are you doing?' shouted Willow.

'If we are to complete our mission, we must find a way out of this godforsaken book room!' she quacked. 'Aha!'

Ted and Willow ran over to look.

Ingrid had found an air vent and was trying to yank the grill off with her beak.

'Go and fetch your ferocious sister,' she said to Ted. 'I could use a bit of her furry muscle.'

Nancy was still sniffing around the trapdoor when she heard Ted calling for her. She dashed back to find him pointing up at Ingrid.

'She's found a way out, sis!' said Ted.

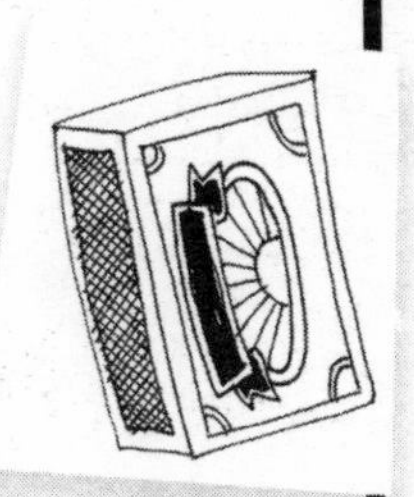

Oh, thank goodness they've found a way out! I was getting **awfully** claustrophobic. But then I am currently trapped inside a matchbox. Um, could somebody let me out please? **Helloooo?**

Everyone blinked a few times as their eyes adjusted to the light and fresh air. Fairy lights were strewn between the tree trunks and wind chimes tinkled in the breeze.

They were in Twinklenuts all right.

'So how do we find the treebonkers, then?' Nancy asked.

'Aha!' said Ingrid, shaking a flimsy-looking plastic box. 'We'll use my foolproof top-secret satellite navigation system.'

Then a spring went boing and a screw came loose and part of the box fell off.

'Oh,' said Ingrid.

And then Willow pointed to a sign that said 'Treebonk practice, this way', which was *very* useful indeed.

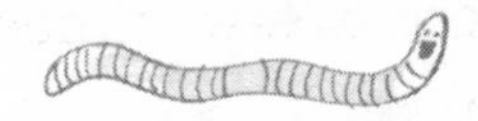

Some minutes later, Willow, Ted, Ingrid and Nancy were hiding in a prickly, thorny bush, spying on the Twinklenuts treebonk team.

'Uh-oh,' said Willow, watching the strong, energetic squirrels do push-ups and shadow boxing. 'This lot mean business.'

They had helmets, shiny leotards and muscles as big as footballs.

The team coach was a weasel who was wearing large sunglasses and lying on a sun lounger.

The treebonkers were amazing. They ran up the tree trunks so fast, Nancy could barely see them. '**Treeebooooonk!**' they cried, pinging themselves from branch to branch like furry pinballs.

'Woah,' said Ted. 'They are GOOD.'

'Yeah. Well, so are we,' grunted Nancy.

But she could see that the Twinklenuts treebonkers didn't seem to be getting tired at all.

Every now and then a squirrel would trot over to one side and take a swig from a silver bottle.

'What are they drinkin'?' asked Ted.

'Looks like energy drinks,' said Nancy. 'Me and my mates used to stay awake for *days* on that stuff. No wonder they ain't getting tired!'

Ted frowned.

'But that's *cheating*,' he said.

Willow started to scramble her way out of the bush.

'I'm going to give 'em what for!' she said. But Ingrid pulled her back in.

'This is not the way to do it, young bunny,' she said. 'We take our time. We watch. We listen. We . . . **QUAAAAAAACK!**'

Ingrid suddenly clasped her wings to her beak. Her eyes grew big.

'Ingrid?' whispered Ted. 'What is it? Are you OK?'

But Ingrid didn't answer. She was staring at something so hard her eyes started swirling around weirdly.

Everyone turned to see what Ingrid was looking at.

And then they saw him.

Another duck had waddled into view and had stopped to chat to the weasel, still lying on his sun lounger. Nancy strained to listen to what he was saying.

'. . . of course, the first play I was ever in ended up running in the West End for *weeks*. Such a surprise! I suppose you could say I was properly bitten by the acting bug, ahahahahaha!'

Ingrid gasped.

'I am in *love*,' she declared.

'Cool it,' said Nancy. 'We have to lie low, you daft bird.' She tried to put her paw on Ingrid to keep her still, but she was too late.

Ingrid waddled over to the other duck as fast as her little legs would go, floofing up her feathers and adjusting her turban on the way. She extended her wing gracefully.

The other duck noticed Ingrid, gasped and took her wing in his.

'Utterly *enchanted* to meet you,' he whispered, taking a bow.

Ingrid giggled shyly and fluttered her eyelashes.

'Allow me to introduce myself,' said the duck.

‘My name is Sir Charles Fotheringay.’

‘And I am Ingrid,’ said Ingrid, who did not need a second name.

‘And what brings a duck as beautiful as you to Twinklenuts?’ asked Sir Charles, his eyes turning into love hearts.

Ingrid giggled again.

‘Oh, just having a wander,’ she said. ‘It really is the most marvellous place.’

‘Have you seen our theatre?’ asked Sir Charles.

‘A THEATRE?’ boomed Ingrid. ‘You must show me at once! For I am a spectacularly experienced actor of stage and screen!’

Sir Charles Fotheringay nodded. ‘I could tell,’ he said. ‘When I saw you, I thought to myself, that duck knows how to tread the boards. Well, we must depart at once.’

‘Ingrid!’ hissed Ted. ‘Come back! What about us?’

Ingrid turned to Ted and gazed at him with her big eyes.

'Young fox! I think I have finally found . . . *my inspiration*!' she said with a swoon.

And the ducks waddled off into the sunset.

Oh, my heart! If I'm not very much mistaken, that was a classic case of love at first quack! I must find my wedding shoes. All **fourteen** of them.

Nancy growled. 'Now Ingrid's waddled off with that fancy pants, it won't be long before Sebastian Silver discovers we're here.'

Ted whimpered.

'B . . . but we can't just leave without Ingrid!' he cried.

'She can look after herself,' said Willow. 'She's a tough duck.'

'I can always come back for her later,' said Nancy. 'For now, let's scram.'

They dropped to the ground and crawled quietly back to the library.

8

CHAPTER ELEVEN
The Whirligig

Nancy was terrible at breaking bad news.

'The duck's gone,' she said. 'She's fallen in love. The whole thing is ridiculous.'

'No! Not Ingrid!' cried Titus, staggering back into his chair. 'I can't believe it! Not only are they stealing our town, they've taken our most famous duck!'

'I'm sure she'll come back,' said Ted. 'She just got overexcited, that's all. She'd never abandon the Grimwood Players! We're her pride and joy.'

'You know nothing of the power of love,

young fox!' wailed Titus. 'When Ingrid falls in love, she falls deep, she falls fast, she falls hard. She's been married FOUR TIMES!'

'Oh,' said Ted.

'And what of Grimwood's finest poet, Emo Omar?' wailed Titus. 'Where is he? Where are his little moley pals?'

'The moles got *well* into the Twinklenuts library,' said Willow. 'We left them by the poetry section. It is pretty cool, to be fair.'

'Everyone really *is* leaving me,' sobbed Titus.

Meanwhile, Frank was worrying about the Twinklenuts treebonk team. Nancy had told him that they were good – really good.

'And you're *sure* you saw them chugging down energy drinks?' he said.

Nancy nodded.

'I'd know them bottles anywhere. That stuff used to keep us up for days in the Big City.

One time my mate Hedge drank three bottles and her fur turned purple.'

The Grimwood treebonk team started moaning and flinging themselves dramatically to the ground.

'It's over! We're done for!' cried Ginger Fiasco.

'We are *never* done for!' scolded Frank. 'Now get up and stand in line. Show me your power poses! I want those Twinklenuts squirrels to be quaking in their leotards.'

The squirrels shuffled about a bit, adjusted their helmets and tried to look scary.

'We're done for,' sighed Frank.

'Hang on,' said Willow. 'Can't *we* just get a load of energy drinks?'

Nancy laughed.

'Those drinks are *hardcore,*' she said. 'We ain't gonna find them around here. Your mate Sebastian Silver must have forked out a loooooot of cash for all those bottles.'

'We need to surprise them,' muttered Frank. 'Something that catches them off guard. A new move, maybe.'

Just then, there was an enormous BANG and an explosion of glitter rained over everyone.

'SORRY!' shouted Pamela from the top of the Magic Tower. She and Sharon the Party Crow were still trying to invent the largest glitter cannon in the world. Volunteers from Bunnyville were signing up to take part in test flights, which meant that every few hours a bunny would fly

through the air in a cloud of rainbow sparkles. This time, it was a chain of three bunnies, who were gripping each other's paws and gliding through the air like a furry plane.

'It's a miracle those bunnies survive,' sighed Titus, shaking the glitter from his antlers.

Nancy looked at Frank, her eyes shining.

'That's it!' she said. 'That should be our move!'

The squirrels looked up at her, confused.

'Aye,' said Frank, also watching the chain of bunnies. 'That could work.'

Frank, Nancy and the squirrels spent the afternoon developing their brand new treebonk move. On Frank's command, the squirrels would grab on to each other's tails and form a long, hairy chain. Nancy – their secret weapon – would go at the very end. Then the chain would spin hard and fast, and Nancy's tail would be able to thwack any enemy treebonkers to the ground.

'What a cool move!' said Willow. 'It needs a name!'

Ted's head rolled round and round and round as he tried to keep up with the spinning squirrels.

'What about the "Whirligig"?' he said. 'Just watching it is making me dizzy!'

Nancy and the squirrels spun round so fast they became a blur.

Frank blew his whistle and the team fell to the ground.

'It's the nuttiest thing I've ever seen,' he chuckled. 'It just might work.'

Reminds me of the time I invented a new move at my local bowling club. If it wasn't for that meddling centipede Janet Muldoon I would have won the championship.

Dang you, Janet!

CHAPTER TWELVE

The day before the day after two days before

It was the day before the match. Everyone had gone wibbly with nerves.

Frank was perched on the bough of a mighty oak tree. Pamela and Sharon the Party Crow were next to him, after Frank reluctantly agreed they could be cheerleaders. It was the final practice session before the big Grimwood vs. Twinklenuts showdown.

'WHOOP WHOOP OH YEAAAAH!' cried Sharon the Party Crow, who was also doing high-kicks, shaking pom-poms and blowing

on a small plastic trumpet.

'Yay, Grimwood,' said Pamela, who was looking at the Treebonk team through a pair of binoculars.

'Remember what we agreed, Pamela,' said Frank in a low voice. 'You are NOT to eat any of the players or spectators, got it?'

'But they look so juicy and hairy,' she sighed.

Frank gave an angry hoot, then turned his head to the treebonk clearing.

'Positions, everyone!' he shouted through his megaphone.

Nancy shot up a tree trunk and waited. She had been exercising day and night. Her tail was the strongest it had ever been.

'READY . . . AIM . . . **TREEBONK!**'

Nancy flung herself out of the tree and pinged between three branches so quickly she didn't even notice she'd knocked two of her teammates to the ground.

'WHIRLIGIG!' shouted Frank.

Thanks to hours of practice, the Grimwood team had perfected their new move. The squirrels linked into a chain formation and whirred dangerously through the air. Nancy's tail was so strong that when it whacked against stuff she didn't feel a thing. Nancy laughed. Twinklenuts were going to get the shock of their lives.

Titus was shuffling about with a broom.

'Tum-te-tum-te-tum,' he was singing to himself – a sign he was massively stressed out. 'Best make the place look nice for our Twinklenuts guests, eh?'

Some beavers in dungarees and hard hats were moving logs around, making a higgledy-piggledy seating area.

'Snacks,' fretted Titus, scratching his antlers. 'Whatever shall we do for snacks? Do I have enough napkins? Oh me, oh my!'

Frank flew over to his friend.

'Chief,' he said gently. 'We're going to be OK. Just look at our foxy friend up there. She's our secret weapon, all right.'

Titus squinted at the trees and saw Nancy treebonking for her life, a streak of bright orange flashing against the blue sky.

He chuckled.

'What a blessing it was, those foxes finding us,' he said to himself.

'We're in with a chance, Titus. I know it,' said Frank. And he folded a wing around his old friend's shoulders.

How heart-warming!

But come, for now we must zoom over to lovely **Twinklenuts**, and very carefully crawl into this old boat.

Ingrid and Sir Charles Fotheringay were floating along the sparkling Crystal Lake in a small rowing boat. Sir Charles Fotheringay was playing a lute quite terribly, while Ingrid was eating grapes and lazily dragging a wing across the water.

‘My love,’ said Sir Charles Fotheringay, ‘you seem distracted. Is anything wrong? Is it my lute-playing?’

Ingrid waved her other wing at him.

‘Not at all, my darlink,’ she cooed. ‘I’m just thinking about my theatre group back in Grimwood. We had SUCH talent, you see. It would be wonderful to show them the marvellous theatre you have here.’

Sir Charles gave a little chuckle.

‘Oh, I’m not sure that would be a good idea,’ he said. ‘My darling Ingrid, here in Twinklenuts we need actors of a certain . . . standard.’

Ingrid bristled. She lowered her sunglasses.

'Are you saying *I* am not an actor of high standards?' she hissed. 'I'll have you know I had a small part in *Motorcycle Bad Guys 3*.'

Sir Charles nodded. 'Oh, I know, darling, I know! *You* are marvellous. *You* are perfect. I'm just not sure about your . . . what do you call them? Your "Grimwood Players". Anyway, once Grimwood is swallowed up into Twinklenuts, well, why even bother *having* them any more?'

Ingrid pushed her sunglasses up and scowled. She suddenly wanted to thwack her new husband in the beak. Only *she* was allowed to be rude about the Grimwood Players. But then she saw the Twinklenuts treebonk team finishing up their practice session in the distance.

'Row that way,' she ordered.

'Anything for you, my darling,' said Sir Charles, and the ducks floated to the shore.

The Twinklenuts treebonk team were taking off their helmets and shaking out their fur.

'Great game, Tobes,' said one of the squirrels, swigging from a silver bottle. 'This super special energy drink really keeps your tail in the air, doesn't it?'

'Yah, totes,' said the other squirrel (who was probably 'Tobes').

'Tomorrow's going to be a walk in the park. Those Grimwood scruffs won't know what's hit them.'

The squirrels chinked bottles and glugged down their drinks.

They did not know that they were being watched by a duck.

An angry duck.

An angry duck who used to be a spy.

The next morning, Nancy woke up and lay staring at the ceiling for a while.

She didn't feel nervous. She felt excited.

She knew Twinklenuts would be a tough team to beat – especially if they were all pumped up on energy drinks. But she also knew that the new Whirligig move could win the match for them. Titus was going to keep his job, and Grimwood would be safe. She could feel it in her bones. She looked over at Ted's bunk. He had already gone to the treebonk arena to get things ready for the big match. There was a card on his bed, ready to send.

Dear Mum and Dad

It's the morning of the massive exciting **treebonk** match! Nancy seems super-cool and relaxed about the whole thing. We are all excited because EVERYONE from Twinklenuts is going to be coming over to watch the match, including Sebastian Silver. He's the mayor of Twinklenuts, and he's a FOX! He's actually kind of cool. Well, apart from his big plan to build a theme park all over Grimwood. But if we win, he promises he won't do it. Phew! I wish you were both here to watch Nancy, but I will do two special cheers from you for luck.

Love
Ted xxx

Nancy shook her head. Her brother always saw the best in everyone – even that slimy old rotter Sebastian Silver. She thought about hearing those two extra cheers from her mum and dad, and suddenly had to do some very fast blinking.

'Right, enough of that,' she said to herself. 'I need coffee.'

Then she heard a noise.

Something had been thrown into the fox den. It was a note, attached to a rock.

She scrambled out to see who had thrown it, but when she popped her nose out of the fox hole, she couldn't see or smell anyone. She went back inside and read the note.

Nancy blinked. This couldn't be true. Could it?

She sat down and examined the note. Her stomach started to flutter.

She had no choice. She had to go. And the match wasn't for hours, so she'd still have time to get to the Magic Tower, come back and warm up.

'If this is a lie,' she growled. 'I'm gonna chew someone's ear off.'

It was spookily quiet up by the Magic Tower. Pamela and Sharon were doing a live broadcast of the radio show down by the treebonk pitch. In fact, most of Grimwood were already there, eagerly awaiting the arrival of the residents of Twinklenuts.

Nancy looked around but she couldn't see anyone at all.

'Hello?' shouted Nancy. 'Who are you, then?'

There was no answer.

'You've got five seconds to show yourself and then I'm leaving, got it?'

Still nothing. Nancy started to count.

'Five . . . four . . . three . . . two . . . one . . .'

BONK.

'OW!' cried Nancy, staggering forward. Her paw reached for the back of her head. She glimpsed a streak of silver just before her eyes closed. And then she crumpled to the ground.

CHAPTER THIRTEEN
Everyone gets a nervous feeling in their tum tum

Nancy groaned and reached for her head. She could feel a big bump.

'She's awake!' she heard someone whisper excitedly.

There was a clatter and the noise of footsteps shuffling towards her.

She forced her eyes open and found that she was somewhere dark and quiet. There were some candles flickering near her.

'Hallo! How are you feeling? You've had quite the bump, I'm afraid,' said a gentle voice.

Nancy slowly turned her head and saw a rabbit. It was grinning a toothy grin and seemed to be missing an ear.

'I'm Mo,' said the rabbit. 'He got to you too, huh?'

Nancy was confused.

A pigeon fluttered onto Nancy's chest and started to examine her with a magnifying glass.

'Gerroff,' said Nancy weakly.

The pigeon bobbed its head from side to side. 'Please, look at my beak. Now follow my beak

this way . . . and now this way . . . and then this way again . . .'

'Urrrgh,' said Nancy.

'Dr Khan, maybe it is best if we let her wake up a little bit more,' said Mo, putting a cup of water gently against Nancy's lips.

'C . . . c . . . coffee?' rasped Nancy.

Some minutes later she was sitting up, sipping on a mug of hot coffee. A crowd had gathered around her.

'Where am I?' asked Nancy.

'You're in Twinklenuts,' said Mo. 'With us! Hello.'

Nancy tried to stand, even though her legs were wobbly.

'I've gotta go,' she said. 'The treebonk match starts soon. I need to get back to Grimwood.'

'Ha!' came a familiar voice. 'No chance of escape, I'm afraid. We've tried.'

Nancy turned and saw a very sad-looking badger. She gasped. It was Wiggy's big brother, Monty. His clothes were all tatty and dirty. Behind him stood Jeremy, Jeremy and Jeremy, all looking very sorry for themselves.

'Woah! What are you lot doing here? Why can't we get out? I need to get out!'

She started to bang on the walls.

'We're locked in,' said Monty. 'That Sebastian Silver chap is a total wrong'un.'

Nancy looked up and realized how full the room was. It was crowded with rabbits, mice, rats, stoats and squirrels. Brown water was slowly dripping out of a tap on one wall, and a large cauldron of soup bubbled away over a fire pit.

'I'm in jail!' cried Nancy. She started growling and looking for an escape route.

'Save your energy, lassie,' said a husky voice. 'Believe me, we've all tried.'

Nancy saw a very old squirrel sitting in a roller skate. He wheeled over to her and held out a paw.

'Crusty McTavish,' he said. 'Pleased to meet you. I was Mayor of Twinklenuts before that horrible crook took over.'

'Woah,' said Nancy. 'Why are you all in here?'

'Silver says we don't meet his so-called guidelines,' said Crusty, shaking his head sadly.

'The Twinklenuts Charter,' said Nancy softly.

'Well, most of us in Twinklenuts couldn't keep up with all his ridiculous rules,' said Crusty. 'So, he shoved us in here! Said that only the "best" (in *his* opinion) were allowed out and about in the new and improved Twinklenuts.'

Nancy couldn't believe her ears. 'But you can't just stay locked in here for ever!' she cried.

'Oh, it's not so bad,' said Monty. 'Especially once you get used to the dark.'

PAAAAAAAAAAAAAAAARP.

'Oh, and Jeremy's awful farting. Try to hold it in, Jeremy!'

'Sorry,' said Jeremy.

'He's told you his grand plan, then?' said Crusty.

'What, building his stupid "Silvertown" resort?' said Nancy. 'Yeah, he told us. Wants to nick the Magic Tower and cover Grimwood with roads and shopping malls and hotels and nonsense.'

'He says when the time comes, he might let us work for him,' sighed Mo. 'Lucky us!'

'Thing is,' scowled Crusty, 'Sebastian Silver always gets what he wants. Even if it means cheating and lying! How do you think he became mayor?'

A rat wearing a broken pair of glasses waved a load of paper at Nancy.

'I'm writing it all down!' he hooted. 'And as soon as we get out of here, I'm going to publish a book called *Fox News: How Sebastian Silver Lied His Way to the Top and Then Locked Loads of Us Up for No Good Reason.*'

'Catchy,' said Nancy.

Just then, there was a quiet *click*.

Nancy looked up.

There was a small hatch in the ceiling. It had whirred open and a load of chocolate bars were dropped onto the floor. It reminded Nancy a bit of the vending machines back in the Big City.

There was a scramble for the chocolate bars followed by lots of noisy chomping.

'Who's feeding you?' she asked, nodding up at the hatch.

'Dunno,' said Mo. 'We never see 'em.'

The hatch slammed shut. Suddenly, Nancy's fur stood on end. A gust of fresh air had swooped down on them as the hatch closed. Nancy's nose was extremely good at picking up scents and it had picked up one in particular. She could smell . . . books.

Ooh, it's all a bit grim isn't it, campers? Funnily enough, I once spent several months in a Swedish women's prison. Got accidentally carried in with some laundry. Quite enjoyed it actually; I made some great pals.

Almost everyone from Grimwood and Twinklenuts had crowded around the treebonk pitch.

'It's the sporting event of the year!' announced Pamela, her voice blaring out from speakers that had been tied to several of the trees.

'OH YEAAAAAAH, **OOOGA WOOOGA BOOOOGA!'** shouted Sharon the Party Crow, dancing and waving some pom-poms in the air. Being an overexcited cheerleader was, in many ways, her dream job.

'Give us a **G**!
Give us an **R**!
Give us an **I**!
Give us an **M**!
Give us a **W**!

'Give us an O-oooooh, are those fizzy cola bottles? Oh, give us a fizzy cola bottle, give us one, give it, give us one.'

Titus, Willow and Wiggy were huddled together in the Grimwood stand. Titus was chewing at his hoof. Wiggy was eating popcorn.

'I know they're the enemy, but they *are* a good-looking bunch,' said Willow, taking in the perfectly turned-out Twinklenuts supporters. 'Also, they smell nice, don't they?'

Titus agreed but he was so nervous all he could say was 'cucumbers!', which was unhelpful.

Wiggy was scanning the glossy-haired crowd, looking for his brothers.

'I can't see the chaps anywhere,' he said. 'How strange! They wouldn't have missed this for the world.'

There was a kerfuffle and then some dramatic quacking.

'Out of my way! Shoo, shoo! Charles, this way please.'

It was Ingrid. She waddled over to the Grimwood stand, dragging Sir Charles Fotheringay behind her.

Willow was immediately furious.

'Urgh, I can smell something HORRIBLE,' she said, refusing to look at Ingrid. 'It smells like TRAITOR.'

Ingrid rolled her eyes.

'Oh, Ingrid!' cried Titus. 'You're back!'

Ingrid nodded.

'Of course,' she said smartly. 'Only a FOOL would leave Grimwood for ever. And I am NO FOOL. Please meet my latest husband, Sir Charles Fotheringay.'

'Charmed,' quacked Sir Charles, extending his wing to Titus.

'We thought we'd lost you,' grinned Wiggy.

Ingrid huffed and shoved herself onto the bench.

'Ridiculous,' she said. 'I fell in love. Is that a crime? You think I would leave the Grimwood Players? You are entirely mad. Now please shuffle along and make space for my husband. **QUAAAAACK!**'

Meanwhile, Frank sat on his special perch pretending not to be worried.

But he was really worried.

Where was Nancy? Without his star player, Grimwood would lose horribly.

'Son, are you sure you haven't seen your sister?' he hissed to Ted, who was anxiously twisting and untwisting his scarf.

Ted shook his head.

'I've been down here all day, Frank,' he said.

'She was asleep when I left home. Do you think she's OK?'

His eyes filled with tears.

'Hush, now,' said Frank. 'We don't want anyone to notice anything's wrong. The team are nervous enough as it is.'

He looked over at the Grimwood treebonk team. They were adjusting their helmets, doing tail stretches and giving each other fist bumps. Nobody could see the Twinklenuts team because they had arrived in a private trailer. Some red velvet ropes had been positioned around it by Susan Kidneys and Fatima Hostile, who were both wearing sunglasses and carrying walkie-talkies. A sign on the trailer door said 'Twinklenuts Only'.

'How long until the match starts?' asked Ted.

'We've only got ten minutes,' said Frank. 'Maybe ask Pamela to do a quick swoop.

If anyone can spot Nancy it'll be her. But make sure nobody finds out Nancy's missing – it'll cause *total* chaos.'

'OK, Frank!' said Ted.

He scampered over to Pamela in the DJ booth and whispered something in her ear. Then Pamela whispered something to Sharon the Party Crow, and quietly swooped high into the air.

Sharon the Party Crow grabbed the microphone.

'OK WHOOP WHOOP, **AWOOGA**! LISTEN UP, EVERYBODY! DJ SHARON THE PARTY CROW IN DA HOUUUUUUUSE!'

There was a cheer from the crowd.

'I'M TAKIN' OVER FROM MC PAMELA,' hooted Sharon, 'BECAUSE SHE'S GONE TO LOOK FOR GRIMWOOD'S STAR PLAYER NANCY WHO HAS TOTALLY GONE MISSING!'

There was a gasp from the crowd.

'Nooooo!' cried Titus.

'Aw, heck,' said Frank.

Most of the Grimwood team fainted.

Just at that moment Sebastian Silver stepped out of the trailer.

The Twinklenuts supporters all started cheering wildly.

'Well, well, well,' said Sebastian, waving at his fans. 'Fancy that. Grimwood's star player has gone missing, eh? What a shame.'

'Oh, man. That's a pity. I hope she's OK,' said Reena, the Twinklenuts team captain. 'That fox seemed pretty cool.'

Sebastian Silver spun around and glared at Reena.

'Er, you want to WIN, don't you?' hissed Sebastian Silver.

Reena nodded.

'GOOD. Because Twinklenuts is only for WINNERS. Now shut up and drink these.'

He shoved a crate of silver bottles towards her with his foot.

'Yes, Mr Silver,' gulped Reena. And she ducked back into the trailer.

Sebastian Silver grinned. Not long now, and Grimwood and its Magic Tower would belong to him for ever . . .

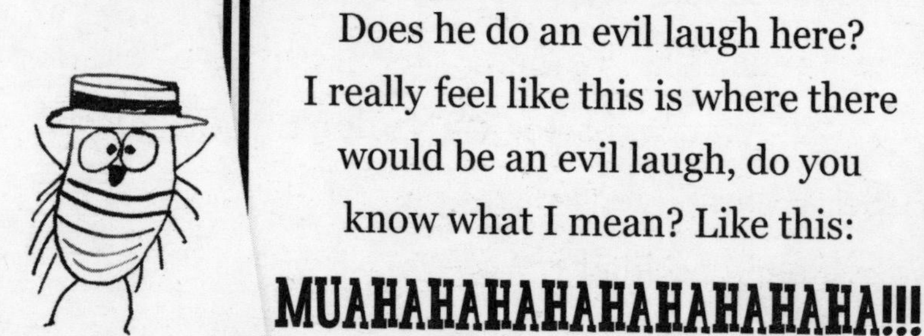

CHAPTER FOURTEEN

The flying of the fur

It was at times like this that Nancy really wished she still had a mobile phone.

'Stupid eagle,' she muttered to herself, remembering how Pamela had stolen it.

'Listen, everyone,' she said. 'I think I know where we are. And if we can get out of this room, we can get out of Twinklenuts.'

Everyone said, 'OOOOOOOH.'

'Are you sure?' asked Crusty McTavish.

Nancy nodded.

'Trust me,' she said. 'But I'm gonna need your help.'

Monty, Jeremy, Jeremy and Jeremy stood to attention.

'Nancy, as you know, we have behaved like total and utter rotters,' said Monty. 'Especially to Wiggy. Any pal of his is a pal of ours. How can we help?'

Nancy snarled.

'Yeah, you've been horrible to him. But you can tell him that yourselves once we get to Grimwood. Now, get me up to that hatch on the ceiling.'

Everyone looked up at the hatch.

She pointed at the badgers.

'You lot. Get on each other's shoulders.'

The badgers gingerly climbed on top of each other, creating a wobbly badger tower.

Everyone gasped as Nancy bravely clawed her way up them, occasionally squishing a

snout or elbowing a tummy.

'N . . . n . . . now what?' shouted up Monty, who was standing at the very bottom, huffing and puffing under the weight of his three brothers and Nancy.

'Now . . . we wait,' said Nancy.

‘Oh cripes,’ said Monty. The badgers swayed from side to side.

‘Keep still down there!’ barked Nancy.

‘Yes, Mummy,’ whimpered Monty.

They waited.

And waited.

And waited.

Then they heard a noise.

The hatch was being opened.

Quick as a flash, Nancy pounced. With one paw she grabbed the edge of the hatch door. It was being opened by a rat in uniform, who just about managed to say ‘Oh!’ before Nancy grabbed him so that he dangled from her paw. She glanced up at the room above her and took a sniff. Just as she thought. They were somewhere deep in the Twinklenuts library.

The rat was twisting around in the air.

‘Let me go!’ it squeaked angrily.

'All right then,' said Nancy, and she dropped the rat onto the prison-cell floor with a thud.

'Come on,' she said to the prisoners. 'We can't wait here all day. Start climbing up and make it snappy.'

The prisoners began to clamber up the ladder of badgers, before reaching Nancy at the very top. Crusty McTavish and some of the older animals were carried up first.

'Holy mackerel!' said Crusty, blinking in the light. 'You did it, Nancy! What a brave and clever fox you are.'

Soon there was a crowd of scruffy, smelly creatures huddled beside the hatch opening. Mo found a tatty old curtain in the library and tore it into strips. Then she tied the strips together into a long rope and hurled it down the hole.

'Here you go,' she shouted. And they hauled

Monty, Jeremy, Jeremy, Jeremy and Nancy out of the secret room.

'What about me?' squeaked the rat. 'I'm really sorry! I promise I was only following orders!'

Nancy just harrumphed and shut the hatch door.

'If anyone sees us walking out of this library, we're done for,' said Mo.

Nancy shook her head.

'There's a secret escape route and it'll take us all the way to Grimwood. Where's the main library room? You know, the one with all the chairs and tables and that?'

Crusty McTavish scratched at his ear.

'I think it's down there,' he said.

The animals shuffled down the corridor.

Nancy noticed a closed door that said '**Map Room**'.

'Hmm,' she said to herself. 'Hang on a

minute, guys,' she called. 'I want to quickly look in here.'

She jiggled the doorknob, but it came off in her paw.

'No probs, Nance!' boomed Monty. 'Stand back, would you?'

And he ran straight into the door, bashing it open with his big badger head.

By the time Pamela flew back to the treebonk stadium, Frank had managed to revive most of the Grimwood team.

'Buck up!' he shouted. 'We can still win. You just have to BELIEVE! Do you believe?'

'YEAH!' shouted back the squirrels.

'We can still do the Whirligig without Nancy, OK? Let's play the best treebonk we've ever played,' said Frank. 'Do it for Titus! Do it for our home! But most of all . . . do it for *yourselves*.'

Titus honked into a handkerchief.

'I'm *so* glad Frank has been coming over for regular movie nights,' he sniffled. 'He's *so* much better at giving speeches now.'

Ted ran over to his friends.

'Pamela said she couldn't see Nancy anywhere,' he said. 'I don't understand it. There's no WAY she'd miss this match.'

'I agree,' said Wiggy. 'She must be in trouble. Come on.'

Wiggy stood up and put his arm around Ted. 'Let's start looking for her while the others watch the match. Might be easier while the forest is quiet.'

'I love you, Wiggy,' said Ted, burying his face into Wiggy's chest for a moment.

Then they ran into the forest.

The Grimwood team huddled together for a last-minute team talk, thumping their tails on the ground.

'Go-go-go GRIMWOOD!' hooted Sharon the Party Crow, and the crowd cheered. All of Bunnyville jumped up and down at once, which felt like a small earthquake. And a stoat called Beryl waved a giant foam paw in the air, like she just didn't care.

The Twinklenuts team were finally outside too, their uniform shiny and perfect, their glossy fur rippling in the wind. Unlike Grimwood, they were completely still and silent.

'They mean business,' said Willow, slurping on a slushie the size of her head.

The Twinklenuts cheerleaders – a group of white mice with pink noses and matching tutus – pranced onto the pitch and did an extremely complicated dance routine involving fire-breathing, juggling and roller-skating.

'I've seen it all before,' yawned Ingrid.

Sir Charles Fotheringay rolled his eyes supportively.

It ended with the mice spelling out the word 'Twinklenuts' with fizzling sparklers in their tails. Then Anoushka Wispy played a pretty song about moths while sitting on a fake cloud.

'Oh, she *does* have the voice of an angel, doesn't she?' said Titus.

'I happen to find her singing extremely bland,' said Ingrid, angrily fanning herself.

But Sebastian Silver was beaming with pride.

'That's our girl!' he said, clapping wildly. 'Isn't she just *perfect*?'

Now it was Grimwood's turn.

Pamela and Sharon the Party Crow trotted onto the pitch. Emo Omar shuffled over from the Twinklenuts stand, looking a little sheepish.

Sharon started to beatbox.

Pamela began to dance like a robotic eagle.

Emo Omar recited his poem.

We jump through the air
And boink the trees with our heads
We fly without care
And hope we ain't deads

Our tails are strong
And we love our 'hood
We're gonna win this game
Yeah they call us Grimwoooood.

(FIN)

The crowd cheered and clapped.

Then Sharon the Party Crow got overexcited and started flapping around the pitch with a disco ball on her head.

'Careful now, Sharon,' cautioned Titus.

'This way, Shazza!' cried Willow.

But Sharon's wrap-around sunglasses meant she couldn't see where she was going, and she wandered into a massive hole.

Sebastian Silver watched the whole thing with one eyebrow raised.

'What an . . . *interesting* show,' he sneered. 'Shall we get on with it, then?'

He looked at Frank, who nodded.

Frank looked at the Grimwood squirrels. 'Come on, team,' he said. 'We may as well give it all we've got.'

The squirrels formed a circle and placed their paws in the middle.

'OOH-OOH-OOH-YEAAAAH!' they chanted.

Frank held the megaphone to his beak. 'Ready . . . aim . . .

TTRREEEEEBOOOOOOOONK!'

The crowd craned their necks as both teams launched themselves into the air. The first few seconds were a blur of flying fur and cries of 'Treebonk!' as the squirrels bounced off branches like hairy ping-pong balls.

'Strong paddle action, Ayesha!' shouted Frank. 'Nice twig grab, Jakob!'

'How is it going?' cried Titus, who had draped a Victoria sponge cake over his face. 'I can't watch!'

'Not bad,' said Willow. 'No

collisions yet, and we're going just as fast as Twinklenuts. Seems like their energy drink ain't working.'

Ingrid tittered behind her wing.

Willow stared at her and started bouncing.

'Did you do a secret spy thing, Ingrid? What did you do, tell me, tell me, tell me, tell me!'

'I replaced their ridiculous energy drink with lake water,' she smirked. 'Somewhere in that lake are some very energetic fish.'

Willow hooted and clapped.

Meanwhile, Sebastian Silver frowned. His team were not boinging as fast as they usually did.

'What's the problem?' he growled at Fatima Hostile. 'Why haven't we won already?

The match has been going on for ten minutes and not ONE squirrel has hit the ground!'

Fatima Hostile shrugged. She was getting a bit fed up. She decided to look for a new job when she got home, maybe one with a nicer boss and proper lunch breaks.

Then a Twinklenuts squirrel tried to yank a Grimwood squirrel to the ground.

'OK, Grimwood!' shouted Frank. 'Let's do it! Time for the WHIRLIGIG!'

Quick as a flash, three Grimwood squirrels linked paws and grabbed their teammate, saving her from hitting the ground. Then they swung themselves round and round, faster and faster, like a squirrel lasso. They smashed into the Twinklenuts squirrel as if it was a conker.

The Twinklenuts squirrel crashed to the ground.

It was a point to Grimwood!

Everyone gasped. Then the Grimwood supporters went wiiiiild.

'We might just do it!' said Willow, bouncing up and down. 'We might just win!'

Five minutes later…

The entire Grimwood team lay face down on the ground.

It was all over.

Twinklenuts had won.

CHAPTER FIFTEEN
A kick in the Twinklenuts

Sebastian Silver threw back his head and laughed.

He strode over to where Titus was sitting. The Grimwood team had collapsed in the corner, their helmets and leotards in tatters. Ginger Fiasco was crying. Willow and Frank were helping the rest of the squirrels get back to their feet. Sir Charles was trying to comfort a wailing Ingrid. Sharon and Pamela had flung down their pom-poms and flown back to the Magic Tower. Meanwhile, the Twinklenuts

supporters were pulling party poppers and chinking glasses of fizzy elderflower.

Sebastian stretched out his paw.

'Well, Titus,' he said, 'a deal is a deal. Kiss goodbye to Grimwood and tell your mad bird to get off my Magic Tower. Well played, chum!'

Fatima Hostile took some sheets of paper out of her briefcase.

Susan Kidneys scrabbled about in her handbag for a pen, and eventually found one, thank goodness.

Ingrid gave an angry quack. 'You are a crook, Silver,' she hissed. 'Please know that I am a vengeful duck and I will ruin your life one way or another.'

Sebastian's eyes narrowed. He leant in, so that nobody from Twinklenuts could hear him.

'Everyone in Twinklenuts adores me,' he snarled. '*Nothing* you say will turn my people against me. You lot had better start looking for somewhere else to live, because none of you will be welcome in Twinklenuts, that's for sure.'

Titus stood up.

'Mr Silver,' he said. 'I have dreaded this day. I have cried many tears. I have eaten many biscuits. But when I became Mayor of Grimwood, I promised to do my job with honour and decency until the end. So, I must accept defeat, because it is right and fair. And that is the Grimwood way.'

With tears in his eyes, Titus held out his wobbling hoof to shake Sebastian's paw.

Just then a voice rang out. 'NO! DON'T SHAKE HIS PAW, TITUS! DON'T DO IT!'

It was Ted. He was running as fast as his little legs would carry him.

Behind him were Wiggy and Nancy.

And behind *them* was everyone who had been chucked into Sebastian's secret prison cell. Crusty McTavish was being wheeled along in his roller skate by Mo.

Ted pointed a shaky paw at Sebastian Silver.

'He's a liar!' he yelped. 'And he's been lying to each and every one of you.'

The Twinklenuts supporters gasped when they saw their old friends.

'It's Crusty! And Mo! And Dr Khan! And loads of others we haven't got time to name!' they shrieked.

'Mr Silver,' said Anoushka Wispy. 'You told us they'd all gone on a really long cruise! Was *that* a lie?'

Sebastian Silver's mouth opened and closed in shock.

'Don't listen to a word this fox says,' said Nancy, jabbing her paw at Sebastian. 'He locked up all these animals cos they didn't fit in with his stupid Twinklenuts Charter.'

Everyone gasped.

'And the so-called official map? It's a FAKE!

We found the proper one in the library. Grimwood ain't even on it – but neither is Twinklenuts.'

Everyone gasped *again*.

Sebastian Silver growled and spun on his heels to face the Twinklenuts supporters.

'I did it all for us!' he shouted. 'Don't you want to see Silvertown become a reality? Don't you want us all to become rich, rich beyond your wiiiiildest dreams?'

'You should never have become mayor,' said Crusty McTavish.

Sebastian Silver let out an evil laugh.

'You're just angry that I won the election, you tatty old squirrel,' he said.

But then Mo held up a large sack. She turned it upside down and hundreds of bits of paper fluttered to the ground.

'Recognize these?' she asked. 'Fake votes

from the Twinklenuts election. We found them hidden in the library. You didn't win nothin'!'

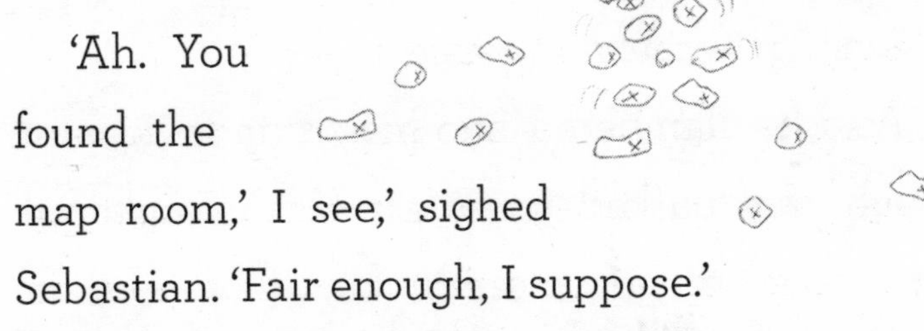

'Ah. You found the map room,' I see,' sighed Sebastian. 'Fair enough, I suppose.'

'He's a FAKE!' shouted Anoushka Wispy, putting down her guitar and sounding very un-wispy.

'He's NASTY!' yelled Reena, taking off her treebonk helmet.

'He's a CHEAT,' said Fatima Hostile, ripping up the papers Titus was about to sign.

And suddenly, it really didn't matter who was from Grimwood and who was from Twinklenuts. Everyone stood together, glaring at Sebastian Silver. He was on his own.

But he didn't seem to care. In fact, he was grinning.

'Ha! Fools, all of you!' he cried. 'Do you think any of you can actually *stop* me? Don't you get it? I can do whatever I want!'

And he clambered into his shiny helicopter, which was parked just next to the treebonk clearing. 'I'm not scared of any of you,' he yelled, as he started the engine. 'I'll take over the Magic Tower whether that stupid eagle is up there or not!'

Ted buried his face in Nancy's fur as the helicopter rose into the air.

The huge, powerful propellers whirred angrily. Sebastian Silver pointed up at them.

'And if your eagle gives me any trouble, she's going to have to deal with *these* bad boys,' he grinned. 'See you later, losers!'

And he steered the helicopter towards Pamela and the Magic Tower.

CHAPTER SIXTEEN

Oops

Luckily, it was just at this moment that Pamela and Sharon the Party Crow finally succeeded in creating the world's biggest glitter cannon.

'*Awooga!*' said Sharon.

'Sparkly-sparkly-boom-boom-boom!' said Pamela, striking a match.

And they set it off just as Sebastian Silver's helicopter appeared in front of them, sending him, the helicopter and a whole load of glitter far, far away into a distant corner of the galaxy.

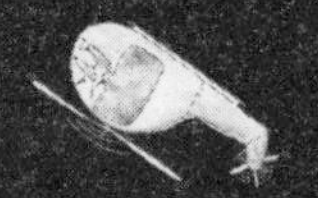

Lawks! I didn't see that coming.

CHAPTER SEVENTEEN
Grimfest

'More pastries, anyone?' asked Titus, setting down a second tray of perfect chocolate eclairs on a large table outside his caravan. He had been baking all week. There were so many more mouths to feed, now that the electric fence between Grimwood and Twinklenuts had been demolished in the glitter explosion. Wiggy was scampering around filling mugs of tea and handing out cups of lemonade. His brothers Monty, Jeremy, Jeremy and Jeremy were helping him.

'You Twinklenuts folk have been through a lot,' said Titus to Crusty McTavish, kindly. 'I hope you know you're all very welcome to stay in Grimwood until you're back on your feet.'

'We ain't posh but we don't have no stupid rules, neither!' said Willow, picking her nose and eating it.

Crusty McTavish wiped a tear from his squirrelly snout.

'Thank you, Mayor Crazyhorns,' he said. 'You've been good to us. Grimwood is a fine, fine place. You should be proud.'

Titus beamed. 'And now that pesky fox is out of the way,' he said, 'maybe Grimwood and Twinklenuts could become *proper* neighbours?'

Crusty McTavish held out his paw.

'Absolutely,' he said.

The glitter cannon had made quite a mess, all things considered. But nobody minded too

much because it had totally saved the day. Pamela had enjoyed seeing Sebastian Silver's helicopter fly into space, and it had been the main topic on her radio show ever since.

Titus had made Sharon the Party Crow a cake of her choosing as a reward, so she had asked for a giant Victoria sponge that she could burst out of at a moment's notice.

Meanwhile, Ingrid, Sir Charles Fotheringay and a quack team of ducks were still scooping glitter out of the Crystal Lake.

'Soon the waters will be clear and beautiful,'

said Sir Charles. 'Though they will never be as beautiful as . . . YOUR EYES.'

'Put a sock in it, Charles,' said Ingrid, scooping up a wingful of glitter. 'You are behaving like a lovesick fool.'

'I've been thinking,' said Sir Charles. 'About your theatre. I should like to rebuild it. Though I know I have the face of a delicate thespian, I have the wings of a hard-working duck. Please, darling? If I am to live in Grimwood with you I shall need A STAGE.'

Ingrid gave a brisk nod.

'Very well,' she said. 'If it makes you happy.'

Though he didn't know it, Charles had just made Ingrid the giddiest duck in town.

'I owe you a big, fat humungous apology, Wiggster,' said Monty the badger. 'And so do Jeremy, Jeremy and Jeremy. We've been rubbish brothers, haven't we?'

'Yes!' said the Jeremys.

'Oh, it's fine,' said Wiggy.

'No, it's not,' said Monty. 'You've been too nice to us and we've totally taken you for granted. Here. I'd like to give you these.'

He handed over a pair of tatty red corduroy trousers.

'My lucky trews,' sighed Monty. 'It's the least you deserve.'

Wiggy gingerly held the crusty trousers and gave his brothers a hug.

Frank was perched high on the bough of an oak tree.

Dr Khan perched next to him.

'The library is next to those cedars,' he said, nodding at a cluster of trees.

'A library!' hooted Frank. 'I've always wanted to visit one of them.'

'It was my favourite place to read the newspaper,' Dr Khan said. 'And occasionally listen to some jazz – with headphones on, of course.'

Frank nodded in approval.

'Maybe . . . maybe we could do that together sometime? In total silence, of course.'

Dr Khan nodded.

'I should like that,' he said. 'It's been very difficult for me these past few years, being surrounded by total nincompoops.'

'I hear you,' said Frank.

After Titus had fed everyone tea and cakes, they all trooped up the hill to gather around the Magic

Tower. Pamela and Sharon were broadcasting LIVE on Radio Grimwood.

'**AWOOOGA AWOOOGA!** You're tuned into Pam and Shazza serving you up a delicious slice of hip-hop, grime and dancehall classics! OH YEAH!'

And they started breakdancing.

Meanwhile, the dreadfully lovely Anoushka Wispy stood up on a battered old crate.

'Hey, everyone,' she said, softly strumming her guitar. 'So, like, we just wanted to say a big thank you to the Grimwood guys for being, like, so amazing.'

All the Twinklenuts animals cheered and clapped.

'And also to say . . . ohmigosh, like have you guys ever tried using soap? It's this fantastic invention that stops your fur smelling like a bin; it's really great. Anyway, here's a song I like to call *"My Toenails Are So Pretty"*.'

Ted ran over to Nancy and gave her a big hug.

'Urgh,' she said. 'What's that for?'

Ted shrugged.

'Felt like it,' he said.

Nancy ruffled his fur.

'How you doing?' she asked.

Ted sighed.

'I'm OK. I feel like a bit of a wally, sis. You know. About Mr Silver.'

Nancy nodded.

'You liked him, didn't you?' she said.

'Only at first!'

said Ted. 'It's just . . . he was a grown-up fox and he looked so *snazzy* and . . .'

'It's OK, kid,' said Nancy. 'I totally get it. We're cool.'

There was a chuckle and the foxes looked down to see Crusty McTavish wheeling past them.

'You're a great pair of foxes,' said Crusty. 'Your parents must be very proud.'

Nancy froze, but Ted just smiled.

'We don't have parents no more,' he said. 'They left us in the Big City and never came back.'

'Oh. I'm awfully sorry to hear that, laddie,' said Crusty, looking a little sad.

'It's fine,' said Ted. 'I've got Nancy. She's the best big sister ever.'

Nancy looked away for a moment. Then she took a deep breath and said, 'We're going to find them, though.'

Ted looked at her in shock.

'There are some paw prints in our den,' added Nancy. 'And my paw fits in one of them perfectly. I need to know if that means something. I need to know who put them there.'

‘Nance!’ cried Ted.

She looked at him and shrugged.

‘I didn’t tell you before cos I didn’t want you to get too excited, bro,’ she said. ‘It might not mean anything.’

‘You know where you should go?’ said Crusty. ‘The library. It’s the best place to start when you need to find something out. Everyone who has ever lived here will have their name written down somewhere. You just need to know where to look.’

‘For real?’ said Nancy.

Crusty nodded. ‘I’d be happy to help,’ he said. ‘It’s the least I can do after you saved our skins.’

‘Yeah, all right,’ said Nancy. ‘That would be wicked.’

Just then, Willow and some of her 345 brothers and sisters whizzed past on tiny bicycles.

'Wheeeeeee!' they cried, riding dangerously fast down the hill, which made their tummies flip. Willow's ears flapped in the wind, and she

was laughing so
much she was dribbling.

'The sun is shining!' she yelled. 'And life is goooooooood!'

And it really was.

Dear Mum and Dad

SO MUCH has happened, you wouldn't believe it! But none of it really matters because Nancy has decided that we are going to find you. I really hope that we do. Did you ever live in Grimwood? Why did you leave us? Are you still alive? I hope so. If you get this, please write back and tell us. I've drawn another map so you know how to get here. You must have a few of them by now I suppose. Whatever happens, I want you to know that we are really happy.

We love you
Ted xxx
Nancy xxx

Crivens! What an escapade that all was. I don't know about you, but I need a holiday. I want a swimming pool, a unicorn lilo and an ice cream as big as my face. **You've been a delight**, I tell you, **a delight.**

I bid you *adieu*!

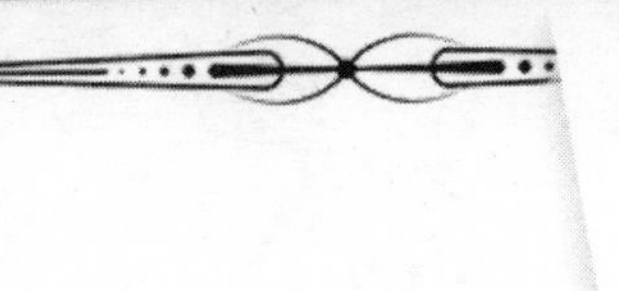

AND
THERE ARE
EVEN MORE
GRIMWOOD
BOOKS
COMING SOON!

NADIA SHIREEN is a bestselling author and illustrator of outrageously funny children's fiction and picture books. She won the UKLA Book Award for *Good Little Wolf* and most recently for *Barbara Throws a Wobbler*, which has been described as a 'little doorway of joy' by Caitlin Moran. She has also been shortlisted for the Roald Dahl Funny Prize and the Waterstones Children's Book Prize, and has been Writer-Illustrator in Residence for BookTrust. The bestselling Grimwood series is her first for older readers, and has been shortlisted for the 2022 Branford Boase Award and the Books Are My Bag Readers Awards. Nadia lives in Sussex.